C.K. SORENS

TRIMARKED

TRIMARKED SERIES
BOOK ONE

This novel contains content that may be triggering.
For a list of possible triggers, please visit
https://www.cksorens.com/trimarked-trigger-warnings

This is a work of fiction. All of the characters, organizations, and events
portrayed in this novel are products of the author's imagination.

TRIMARKED

Edited by Whitney O. McGruder

Cover design by www.OriginalBookCoverDesign.com

www.cksorens.com

ISBN 978-1-954054-00-4 (paperback)
ISBN 978-1-954054-01-1 (ebook)

First Edition: December 2020

To you.
Because of you, this story won't just live in my head anymore.
Now it can live in yours.

1

EMBER

*E*mber Lee stood elevated up the hill from the Trifecta High throng where they congregated at the End of the World. The serpentine road curved through the forest, a sunken river of asphalt that led from the gridded streets of Town. For the last mile, broad Redwood pines and dense brush grew next to the raised shoulders, blocking out the sights and sounds of all they knew. The road drifted in lazy, descending arcs and directed a wandering eye to city lights in the valley below, a place far, far away and just as impossible to reach as a fairy-tale castle.

Animals passed this point without struggle, and vegetation grew as if all were well. A person stopped as if hitting a glass door that declined to break. A car would crash, hood crumpled, with no damage to be seen in the barrier's emptiness. Attempts to use small stones to line the dome failed when the wind or other force pushed them until they rolled on through and escaped, not bound by the same rules. No one wanted to set a concrete marker. A long-term solution unsettled Trifectans who didn't want this trap to prove permanent.

Though the barrier encircled the entire town, the End of the World was special. This spot was the most accessible within human territory, and the last place where a road met the barrier, all other intersections destroyed over the past two decades by the encroaching forest or by purposeful demolition. A 'Now Leaving' sign on the shoulder was a mocking reminder that people had once traveled unhindered. Had it been reachable, crowds like the one gathered now would have mutilated the rectangular declaration. Instead, it stood a few feet beyond an energy so strong no person had ever forced their way through, and the white metal remained steadfast, aged only by fading letters and small bites of rust.

The sign mocked those who approached, fed negative sparks into the charged atmosphere. The End of the World pulsed with raw intensity that burned from the deepest places of being told "You Can't."

You can't have the same freedoms as your parents. No cell phones. No TV channels beyond the town's one, no chance to surf that complicated thing called the internet. All your information will come from old books, because you can't get new ones, not for your homes and not for your school.

You can't drive the road as it recedes into the east, an arrow to the forbidden freedom of the city lights seen on the lowered horizon. A solid, invisible wall stops you. The same magic that pushed the Witches and Fae into the human realm and trapped the races together, forced to coexist, compelled to accept the end of travel.

You can't visit the north and east, because that is where the mages live. Forced from their realms into this one with the barrier's birth, an agreement between the classes split the land. The Laws of Convergence allow for movement between the territories, sure, but going beyond Town takes you from the comfort of humanity and into the suspicious cultures of magic.

Fae and Witches hadn't existed in the human realm of Terra before the Fade. Fae had lived in Gypsum and the Witches had Heldu, realms that shared the Earth, though on different sides of the same page. Two decades ago, the Veil between them malfunctioned over the town of Trifecta. Fae and Witches living in the same space within their realms were forced from home and into the human realm. The Veil hardened, creating an impenetrable bubble around Trifecta where all three races found themselves trapped, and forgotten.

Twenty years was long enough to become complacent and accept life had changed, and to acknowledge the outside world seemed to have forgotten their small mountain city.

A million years would never be enough to stop the yearning, to stop the desperate hope that one day the invisible, impenetrable barrier would fall.

Ember wrapped thin arms around herself to protect her narrow frame against the evening chill. Long black hair encircled her neck, secured under the ties of her multiple sweater hoods. She used the massive Redwood to cut off any gusts of wind and wished she'd put on another pair of socks. It was quieter up here, the heavy forest able to muffle the music and shouts from the party. Nothing blocked the shared sense of need, and that pissed her off. She didn't want to share a fading thing with those humans, or admit they might be the same. Yet, she kept watching.

Vehicles parked on the pine-needle covered shoulders, backed up against the rise of the forest. Headlights angled along the road from each side, past the barrier, and flooded the asphalt like a runway. High beams that didn't bounce off the end of town sign sent a cloud of light into the nothingness over the drop of the small mountain's decline. They back lit the teen rockstar playing the young crowd. His fists thrust into the onyx sky to encourage cheers. Drivers tuned their car radios to the same station to play the same song, pulsing bass into the night.

The boy on the runway stretched his chest with a few elbow thrusts behind him, then shot over the last patch of level ground. A few steps before the descent, he leaped high, turned his shoulder to the moon and slammed into the thick air of the barrier with silent impact. His rebound crash to the pavement and consequent moan drowned under the approval of those around him, even though the magical dome remained.

"Man, you took that hard!"

"I bet that was the highest jump. Hey, who's keeping track?" The different greetings and accolades floated to Ember's chilled ears.

"Bouncers." Chase whispered the slur from close behind her.

"A lot like us, standing here in the cold, just watching," she shot back.

Chase's lanky form stood out from the lighter shadows as he slipped past her. "Let's go, then."

Four others appeared in pairs. The group was composed of Halfers, people who claimed blood from two races, all human, some Witch, some Fae. Mixed-race kids were unwelcome beyond their outcast, underground community, nicknamed such because of their ability to hide between the cracks.

The Halfers' preference for segregation from the "normal humans," or topsiders, proved mutual. The town was too small for a person to take on a false label and identity equalled status. One could not claim topside humanity without a parent to support that, a friend to insist on it, a family to document it.

Parents of the Halfers could become outcasts themselves, an admittance of an unwelcome relationship between the races. So, instead they hid their pregnancies and either tried to hide their offspring, or 'gift' them to the underground community where the topsiders thought they'd be more welcome. Sometimes babies passed off in the shadows struck a memory of abandonment in the new caregivers. Every once in a while, privileges the topsiders enjoyed that they didn't have irritated the Halfers, such as caring parents and car usage. On those nights, members of the underground found solace in taking away a few of the topsider's toys.

If Halfers were capable of magic, no Fae or Witch parent

came forward to share knowledge with them. Human parents were the same. Halfers had become resourceful borrowers and thieves, and had their own forms of education that allowed them to get back at the topsiders just fine.

"Old gasoline vehicles had loads of ways to disable them. Electrical, potato in a tailpipe, sucking out fuel."

Ember checked out the speaker. He was twelve years old and on his first prank, trembling despite his coat. Ember had started with the crew at the same age and five years later her heart rate maintained its steady rhythm during Chase's fun and games.

Keegan stopped the kid's lecture with a heavy hand to his nape. "Keep sucking tailpipes to yourself and you'll be fine. All we need are these." Keegan's wide shoulders loomed as he tossed altered cell phones and twisted cords to Chase and the last pair of the crew. Though mobile service was part of Trifecta's past, limited resources resulted in using everything still left. An old phone was a handheld computer and angry outcasts made the best hackers.

"Should you be caught, we blame it all on you." With a parting evil grin, Keegan took the new kid in tow and circled around to cross the street. Ember allowed herself a returning smirk, knowing the darkness hid it.

"We start at the far end of this side." Chase shimmied underneath the last vehicle, an 8 seater van.

Ember jimmied the charge port. Chase extended the plastic encased cord for her to grab and fit into the outlet. Not an exact match. She had to hold it and keep watch while Chase uploaded a bug that would make the battery appear drained the moment the vehicle shifted into drive.

A petite girl with an oversized pom pom on her knitted hat showed off her straddle jump. Another ovation followed by a groan and the crowd demanded the next person bust through or break their bones trying.

Time would be up when the last kid jumped. If they didn't

finish, Ember wouldn't get paid. Chase was the only one who traded with her and her mother in this town of limited resources. She couldn't chance going home empty handed. Chase's pranks weren't what she considered work, but he claimed it was effort worth paying for. With her cut being a bag of food, that was all the reason she needed to join the crew for an evening.

"Done," Chase said.

Ember tossed him her end of the cord, shut the charge port, and crept along the line to repeat the process. With four cars bugged and the fifth begun, she caught the sound of footsteps on gravel, then a longer slide and a surprised gasp when somebody slipped.

"Verge," he cursed. "Brandt, why did you push me?"

Aaron Harwell. His perfect house sat a few yards down the road from hers. Their usual habit of ignoring each other might change if he spotted her vandalizing. Chase pressed the phone closer to his chest to hide the light, signaling he was not willing to abort. She peeked over the hood of the car to guard against the humans' progress.

"Just making sure you didn't break anything. Maybe not the best idea to rush into the barrier at ground level," Brandt said.

"As opposed to what everyone else is doing?"

"You bounce off it softer the higher you get."

"Says who?" Aaron asked.

"Fade, man, what's your problem?"

Aaron grumbled something in response as their footsteps landed on the other side of the vehicle. Chase shimmied under the car to hide, one sport pants clad leg extended from the hem of his tunic length hoodie.

Dedicated to the end. Fine. Ember adjusted her grip on the cord to maintain the connection. If she didn't hold it steady, they would have to begin again, or abort. Chase's plan did not include giving up.

Ember rose from her crouch, and leaned against the evidence. Her presence drew the human boys' attention. To ensure she had their entire focus, she eased off her hoods to release her long, black hair, trying to look calm.

Brandt stumbled with her sudden appearance from behind the car. He glared at her and recovered, chest thrust forward as if he wanted to prove he could tower over her and stay six feet away. Brandt's fashion twin with a Trifecta High letter jacket and dark jeans, Aaron's taller frame side-stepped in front of him, massaging the upper part of his left arm.

"It's the Trimarked girl," Aaron soothed. Brandt straightened in surprise and peeked around the sandy curls atop Aaron's head. Ember's lips quirked in a self-deprecating smile. Right. The Trimarked girl.

Human mom. Witch dad. Born on Fae soil. The worst offenses anyone could make prenatal, and the only of her kind.

Brandt lugged a thick, mucus-filled wad of saliva across the hood. Ember twisted to avoid it while struggling to keep the off-size cord connected to the car's larger port. The spit landed in a weighted glob on her shoulder. The smell alone had her face turned away, arm angled back. A slight pinch flickered over the hand holding the connection and she hissed, betting she'd caused a spark with the jostle.

"What are you doing here?" Brandt spoke as if his kind owned the world. Ember smiled.

"Taking bets on who gets the worst concussion."

"Holy shit, the mutt talks." Ember's shoulders stiffened at Brandt's insult. She kicked toward Chase to urge him to hurry.

"Multiple languages," she offered. Aaron winced as he rolled his shoulder.

"She isn't worth it. Her guardian--" he tried, but guys like Brandt....

"Barking ain't a language." Not even clever. Ember wasn't paying attention to his words. She tracked the way his feet crossed over each other, how he knocked Aaron's hand away as he passed his friend. "And she isn't worth a lick of spit."

Chase tugged at the cord. She dropped it, slipped her leg from his gentle grip on her ankle and met Brandt's firm footed steps.

"Oh, so you want this back?" Ember swiped the horrid smelling slime and slapped it across Brandt's scratchy cheek. Brandt's rage cooked deep within him. His reaction was slowed by drink, and allowed her to step closer to slam her knee into his crotch. He doubled over, which made it easy to lean forward, grab his wavy brown hair and smash his face into the hood.

But guys like Brandt never go down unless it's in flames. He burst upright, twisted from Aaron's attempt to restrain him, ignored the blood flowing from his nose and reached for her. His fingers brushed her hoodie, but missed. Ember redirected fight energy into flight up the inclined shoulder, determined to reach the forest.

A tree split in two. Ember didn't adjust fast enough and crashed into a hard, hot torso covered in a tailored wool sweater. She inhaled pine and mist in a warm pocket of air. A shudder wrapped around a bone deep quiver as familiarity with the scent clashed against the foreign feel of contact.

Heavy hands decorated with smooth, curved tattoos pressed on her upper arms. He maneuvered her against the trunk as if she were a piece on a game board. Not a friend, yet not unwelcome at this moment, Nicu put her in her place and turned his back so her view settled on tight layers of long, narrow box braids as he faced the boys down the hill.

Shock was the only reason she stayed, she told herself.

Shock and a little thrill at what would come next for that jerk who thought he could spit on her.

2

NICU

*N*icu Coccia did not have time for distractions. He must manage them, regardless, especially when they came in the form of chaos embodied, otherwise known as the Trimarked Child.

Using his body, Nicu barricaded the hybrid girl from her attacker, a menacing warning banked in his amber eyes. Brandt scrambled in retreat to the car. His hand slipped on the bumper before he hauled himself to his feet.

"Hey, give us a chance to explain," Aaron said, placing a hand on his friend's shoulder.

Nicu used the play of shadows and light, angled his jaw and furrowed his brows, pushed thick sleeves up muscled forearms to display long, curved lines of Living Ink, tattoos one shade darker than his skin. A twist of his wrist made the rolling pattern appear to move. The boys flinched back.

As if he'd waste any genuine power on the pair.

"Leave her be," Nicu demanded.

"What the hell," Brandt argued.

"You didn't see who attacked first."

Nicu turned to Aaron with those words, saw the human's eyes focused on the shadows behind him, toward Ember.

Whether to shift the blame or gain support, neither would work. They should at least believe their own rumors that he guarded the girl at all times, should assume he was aware of what they'd done.

"Bullies have a way of twisting the truth."

Aaron's attention refocused where it should be, on Nicu. The human's jaw clenched. He rubbed his arm, no doubt a souvenir of their stupid weekend rally.

After a last long assessment of the two friends, one hurt and one drunk, Nicu let his features relax, his eyes hood, then turned away. The message: They were not worth his time.

"Verge, Brandt, learn when to stop," Aaron hissed and returned his friend to the party.

One more distraction to handle.

The hybrid child stood rigid as the tree, fingertips against the bark as if that contact alone had kept her still. Of course she stayed. Nicu hadn't said she could leave.

The Fae had long since placed him in charge of her, responsible for keeping her under control and to report if the worst were to happen. A human interaction was minor, yet dangerous. If she'd felt truly threatened, there was a chance she'd reach deep, find something she should not touch, defend herself with it regardless of the consequences. A display of High Magic, a potential effect from being born on Fae soil.

Fae magic was two sided. Their main abilities aligned with Nature. They dove deep within the physical to extract magical atoms and produce elegant Works of function and beauty.

As an extension, Fae manipulated an equally magnificent and infinitely dangerous power. High Magic allowed them to delve into space and time, manipulate events and emotions. To do so was to court chaos, to risk kingdoms falling, volcanoes erupting, lives ending, and worlds cracking apart.

Fae had once thought that by controlling themselves, their communities, and their magic, they could control the effects of High Magic. They had been wrong. Once, all people, mage and human, had lived in the same realm, but owning magic became a dreadful and dangerous difference between the peoples. The Fae had delved too deep in order to protect themselves. The world broke, and split it into the three realms of Terra, Heldu and Gypsum.

Each race became bound to their one dimension. Fae and Witches learned to part the Veil and visit Terra at will, though never for too long as the energies of Terra did not support magic. That had been their existence for thousands of years until the anomaly of two decades past. The malfunctioning Veil had forced coexistence again, if only in this small pocket of a town.

After the cataclysmic event that split the realms, the Elders had forbidden most High Magic. Those not outlawed remained secrets of the Fae, and only Worked by a master with a lifetime of practice and control. Seventeen years ago, such a spell had been used to stop the birth of an aberration, the Trimarked Child. The caster failed. The ricochet of power had killed two members of the Fae, and left two others forever mutated, Nicu included.

The two sides of Fae magic were inseparable. If the Trimarked Child showed signs of one, she would be capable of both. If she held Fae magic within her, she certainly contained Witch powers from her father. Fae magic on its own could rewrite the history of a world. Add Witch magic and the capability for destruction was unimaginable. And it would mean destruction. Her human blood would be a disability. Humans could not sense or manipulate magic. The enhanced control required for Fae magic was beyond her. The Trimarked Child was a bomb without a switch.

Such powers might never manifest, but the Fae did not believe in leaving things to chance. The Binding Ink at her neck worked to limit access to her potential abilities, a pin in her grenade. Chaos was unpredictable, however, and so the Fae had charged Nicu with overseeing the hybrid girl.

Nicu found his job more akin to a keeper. He kept her in check, kept her from becoming noticed in a place all knew of her and her forbidden birth. And he made sure everyone within Trifecta knew and understood, she was untouchable.

"Reckless." He moved into the surrounding silence, leaving the party behind the last line of trees.

"Oh, I wouldn't say that. You appear to have had yourself in complete control."

Nicu stepped up the hill, though careful not to get too close. He wanted her cowed enough to listen, not frightened into fighting. She tilted her chin.

"You let him notice you," he said.

She flinched, turned her head away. Good.

"You let him talk to you."

"Damn it, Nicu," she rasped. "I'm not invisible. People can have a conversation with me."

"Stop being difficult."

"You have no idea."

Irritation flared in Nicu's gut, drew him further into her space. She did not appreciate the sacrifices he made to keep her under the radar, did not recognize how being inconspicuous could be a shield. In defiant declaration, her silver crystalline eyes remained immovable against his. He advanced and raised his hand an inch at a time, slipped it under the heavy fall of inky hair and pressed two fingers against the back of her neck.

Her body shuddered in concession, knowing what he meant by the contact. A reminder of the dark Binding Ink placed there by Fae long ago. A pentacle centered on her spine with a half butterfly on the right. The star had an angled line across it, to break her connection to magic, and to make sure everyone remembered the violation of her birth. A magical binding to stop her from accessing what he, too, monitored in her. The Trimarked Child's unknown power. The only reason she was allowed to walk free was because of this mark and his guardianship.

She could not afford to forget, even for a moment.

"You travel too close to your boundaries. Control yourself."

"Like you?"

"Little hybrid," he murmured, marking the reactive flicker of her eyelashes. "Right now, you are contained. You live as you wish." Ember opened her mouth to argue. Nicu's chest pressed within a centimeter of hers to steal her breath and stop her words.

"Become a nuisance, and you will find out how being controlled feels. If you turn dangerous…" Nicu's amber-glass eyes cut into her defiant angles until the edges of her softened, then dissolved on a heated sigh.

"Never forget, little hybrid, the Fae are the reason you are alive. They can change their minds."

Her gaze dropped.

Nicu removed his hand. With slow, deliberate action, angled his body to open a path for her. The chill air turned frigid in place of the heat between them, but he did not allow her to see how it affected him. He noted her gasp at the shift. She had such little control.

"Go home. Now."

The hybrid child huffed and pulled her hood back up against the cold and him. He watched long enough to make sure she walked in the right direction, up the slope toward the layered streets of human households. Satisfied, he melted into shadows. Another night, he would follow her the whole way, but tonight he did not have time.

While trailing the Child and her dubious companions as they moved from the underground to the End of the World, there had been a disturbance in the magic defining the Fae border. Nicu was tied to the spell and his unit was tasked with responding to any unexpected manipulations immediately. His primary task of monitoring and managing the hybrid girl had delayed him. He needed to make up time. A clash of duty was not an acceptable reason to fail at either.

Nicu rushed north between ancient pines, away from the human portion of Trifecta and toward the Fae's one-third fraction of the land. Moss-covered stone increased in regularity as the slope elevated, and he dodged boulders as often as trees. Feet bounced off the needled floor, shifted around thin branches to keep the dry wood from snapping under his tread. In his tenth year, magic had been used to substantially enhance his vision, so now he could separate shapes in the complete darkness of forested midnight.

"You were too nice to the gulls." Edan joined on his right, using the Fae slang for the screeching, gullible humans. The second of their unit pulled a knitted hat the same chocolate color as his eyes over his shaved head and buttoned his fitted wool coat to the top even though it restricted movement in his shoulders.

"You were too lenient with the Child." Branna shared her opinion from Nicu's left, her signature black harmonized with the nighttime forest. Nicu clenched his teeth on a sigh against their complaints.

"We need to focus on our current task."

"To meet a Witch." Edan's Fae training provided him enough control to keep the challenge from his tone. Still, Nicu noticed it in a subtle shift of muscle, in the tenor of his stride.

"To investigate a border breach," Nicu countered, though the theory was sound, as it was unlikely caused by a human, and Fae knew how to avoid triggering the spell.

The Laws of Convergence allowed free travel within Trifecta, though the truth was more complicated. Trust spread thin between the different communities. To guard against unexpected visitors, no matter their intentions, both the Fae and Witches marked their boundaries with spells tied to unique vines, heart shaped leaves for Fae, triangular leaves for

Witches. Not solid like the barrier, the magic acted more as an alarm system warning of trespass.

Though Nicu didn't know for certain how the Witches managed their boundary, he was the lone Fae attached to theirs. Nicu needed to be hyper-aware for a moment the Trimarked Child attempted entry. The Elder Council had banished her from their territory and even an accidental crossing would not be tolerated.

Nicu would not abide breaking his oath to his people, or to the Promise Magic that bound him. He'd ensured Ember understood the gravity of the consequences if she tried to enter Center, which left to question who disturbed the boundary now.

"Assumptions can be traps," Nicu warned Edan. "Devi may be the only one to use border manipulation to date, but the location is wrong, as far from their land as possible."

"She likes us at her beck and call," Edan defended his theory.

"I want to learn how she avoids our patrols, no matter her whereabouts," Branna said.

"And what secret of value are you willing to trade?" Nicu's question resulted in the reaction he'd hoped for. Silence. The trio fell in and with less breath wasted, they increased their pace to reach the place human land ran into Fae along the confines of the outer barrier. They avoided the hunting parties, careful not to scare away any game. Though this was human territory, the Laws of Convergence gave Fae permission to hunt, sell the meat at market and keep plenty for themselves.

When they reached the border, Devi was not in attendance.

The cause of the disturbance proved to be a tall figure wrapped in heavy folds of delicate, woven yarn in deep purples and lighter blues, balanced and alternated into the particular pattern his ancestors had worn for generations. Pale moonlight reflected off silvered locs tied together at his nape where they twisted in a thick cord along the length of his spine.

Unadorned fingers danced on the air as if considering another brush against the heart-shaped leaves, then retreated in decision.

Though not forbidden for a Fae to trigger the border alarm, this proved unexpected and personal. Nicu hesitated a moment, then turned to study Branna's drawn features.

"Go to the Child's house. Be my eyes there."

Branna disappeared between one tree and the next, a sign of how happy she was to avoid contact with their summoner.

"I will be your ears." Edan scaled a pine to find a high perch.

Mindful of his breath, Nicu slid beside the figure. His steps remained on human territory. Wist stood within Fae lands.

Their feet edged against an eroded cliff, a sudden drop in the otherwise gradual decline of the mountainside. A weathered landslide provided the Fae with a view of the valley. The quarter moon shone bright in the blue-grey darkness, the trees a bumpy spill of darkest ink. Scattered stars glinted across the vast sky, more of their tiny lights struggling through time and space as the two men watched.

Fading into Terra had affected the Fae more acutely than it had the Witches, a fact kept hidden as magic forced them to fade in and out of Terra. After three years of pushing them through only to allow them back home, the power had fluctuated one last time. The bubble in the Veil that caused the anomaly had hardened in a way never seen or recorded in centuries of history.

The territory they had claimed while drafting the Laws of Convergence was the one place in Trifecta that held echoes of Gypsum energy. Pure Fae preferred not to leave the familiarity they found concentrated within the old campground, leaving Wist's visit steeped in questions.

"Twenty years, Nicu." Wist, senior member of the Fae Council, breathed hot frustration into the air. "A hand span of time that has felt like an eternity while stuck in Terra. Not that you understand."

Wist's muttered words dripped with meaning. A reprimand for Nicu's delay and a reminder of his inferior status, not just because of age but due to birthplace.

As the first Terraborn, Nicu was the oldest of a new, lower class of Fae. They made up an entire generation of those born in this realm. Fae who never had the chance to absorb the true essence of Gypsum. Nicu had to work hard to prove himself competent, to always follow orders no matter the personal cost, to nurture complete control. Even putting him in charge of the Trimarked Child did not mean they trusted him. They did not want to spread the contamination. He was already affected, and they knew him capable of the job.

"It's disappointing you haven't realized, especially with your history." Wist said with a quiet tsk. "The Ternate rises again."

The segments of Nicu's spine solidified, his chest widened and limbs lengthened with the pressure of the moment. A thumb's breadth from the horizon, he saw it. That which appeared to be one bright star was a group of three, bound in conjoined orbit. The last time they peaked into the sky was the night Ember Lee had been born.

"You are aware of what the Ternate means." Nicu jerked a nod toward Wist's unwelcome statement. Known as the Chaos Star, the Fae reviled the cursed Ternate, a dreaded harbinger of change. "It will test us, test the interior safety measures. Observe the humans to see if they pay more attention to mages, or if they remember buried fears and original claims. Those will be the first signs."

The humans remembering and reacting more would be tell-tale markers that the Fae defenses were weakening. Spells cast over time to ensure the persecutions of the past would not resurrect in a culture as unpredictable as it was reckless. Guns fired off faster than incantations. A dampening of human aggressions had been deemed paramount to Fae safety, a measure the Witches had not fought, either. They, too, remembered the witch hunts.

"I understand, Elder Wist."

Wist turned to study the younger Fae for a time. Nicu kept his features calm and flat. That he didn't give absolute compliance wasn't the problem. Fae rarely committed to agreements and preferred to leave room for adjustment as necessary. What Wist looked for, Nicu couldn't tell, but he hoped the elder ended up satisfied.

"Another thing. I thought you were tied to the power of the barrier?" Features as blank as Wist's, Nicu internalized his surprise.

"I am able to sense its energy, just as any other magic." Each word slow, calculated. Wist's attention narrowed.

"Then have you realized someone has been testing it?" Wist leaned in and Nicu kept his breath flowing and his pulse steady so the Elder could perceive nothing from a change in cadence. "From outside Trifecta. A matter of importance with the presence of the Chaos Star."

Knowledge Nicu did not have, including the question of how the councilman knew what happened beyond their side of the thin, impenetrable Veil.

"Keep me apprised of any changes. With luck, the stars won't shine their light here with this rising. If not.... I trust you to come to me. I will see you at Center."

One set of footsteps disappeared, and another approached him.

"You heard nothing of the external disturbance?" Nicu asked. Edan stripped off the knitted hat. Porcupine quill tattoos peeked up his neck.

"No, but that should change soon."

Frustration shimmered through Nicu and he tempered it by focusing on the star.

"And what of Wist's visit?"

"There were no whispers of movement. This may have been a spur-of-the-moment decision."

Nicu tucked the information away. It wasn't enough to know what the Elder was up to, though it aroused suspicion that he acted without the council's knowledge.

An uncontrolled tremor proved a poor warning. The air before him shimmered and shifted. A hazy mist jumped off the surface of the barrier, a temporary visual sign of its existence. A slight wave drifted through the focused energy, warped the dome. The backlash of power pressed against his core like a stiff breeze until it forced him to take a large hop back or risk a fall. As soon as it began, the flare stopped, no natural disbursement of gentle ripples.

His stomach sank. Nicu recognized the disruption. A power from within Trifecta caused it. What chilled him now was he'd never seen the shape of the bubble shift and roll with such force, and this time he wasn't the only witness.

Nicu's heartbeat doubled.

"Nicu." Edan's voice was sharp in concern, a shock to help Nicu regain composure.

"Did you sense it?" He studied the nuances of Edan's reaction, not sure how much to disclose, even to his second. Edan absorbed the words, shifted away from the spirit of them.

"Was it a fox hole?" He asked, referring to the stumble instead of the query. He had not detected the rush of power or seen the barrier react.

Nicu allowed himself to breathe easy. To the other Fae, nothing had happened. The Trimarked Child would be safe.

Now to get her under control.

"Find her."

Edan did not mistake who.

"You sent Branna after her."

Nicu paused, decided in the next breath this offer of knowledge to be worth the price.

"Branna went to her house. The Child did not."

"It would be easier for you." The comment questioned how Nicu knew Ember had not gone home.

"Edan," Nicu snapped. "She is somewhere along the barrier. Go. Now."

Nicu turned toward the calm space beside him with Edan's departure. He reached out, then pulled back, not ready to find out if the boundary still held.

Duty could not be avoided, no matter his trepidation. Nicu's palm flattened against the steady energy. With both hands raised at shoulder height, he shoved. Nothing gave.

Nicu's eyes burned. He looked past the drop and saw the Ternate. Lashes lowered to brush the top of his cheeks and his forehead dropped. His full weight leaned against the nothingness as he hoped the erratic pulse of magic had little to do with Ember.

3

AARON

*B*randt's shove didn't move Aaron, but the momentum sent him a sidestep too far and he corrected with an exaggerated weave of his body.

"What was that, Aaron? You're the captain."

"Of a soccer team," Aaron agreed, wondering what that had to do with him preventing a fight with Nicu and Ember after Brandt made a colossal ass of himself. Brandt's actions pushed the line tonight. If he'd pulled that shit with another human, Aaron wouldn't have put up with it. Lately, Brandt tested a lot of limits. Aaron frowned against a headache and wished his friend would work out whatever bothered him.

"Best friends since fourth grade," Brandt said.

With a meeting not too much different from tonight. Ten-year-old Brandt had started a fight during recess outside their large K through 12 school building. The argument was over who won the monkey bar race. Aaron stopped fists from flying and helped prevent Brandt's expulsion. Brandt had been grateful, once he'd calmed down, and a lopsided friendship began.

"Which means I keep you away from trouble," Aaron replied.

"We're two of the biggest guys in school. It was one Fae

and the skinny Trimarked bitch." He wiped dried blood from his nose with a wince. The pain added to the heated steam on his face.

"You scared of a little pixie?" Brandt demanded. Aaron wondered if his friend's drunken haze allowed him to truly see the Fae who had inches on either of them, both in height and bicep.

"I don't want to figure out if we can take him after you've had four cups."

Brandt muttered about making it five as he staggered away, beer the main reason Brandt attended these End of the World parties. Aaron came to hang with the soccer team and blow off steam by beating up the barrier. Though they never broke through, Aaron liked to imagine they produced as many invisible bruises on its surface as it left on their skin.

Before Brandt reached the folding tables where the beer and food were set up, Aaron made eye contact with Jose, defensive midfielder, key and keg keeper. Aaron sliced a hand across his neck with a nod to Brandt. *Cut him off.*

Jose returned with a brief salute and Aaron relaxed his shoulders, winced again at the one he'd jammed against unforgiving air. He tracked Brandt's approach to where Jose guarded the beer, a weaker brew his dad made in his basement for the high schoolers. Jose's dad saved the stronger stuff for the adults. A few teens thought low alcohol content meant they could drink more. Jose let them know differently with a hard shake of his head and a refusal to refill a glass.

Aaron watched long enough to make sure Brandt's drunken tantrum involved only a few shoves and shouts. Brandt beat up a pine tree before he staggered into the forest. Aaron relieved himself of the responsibility.

Brandt needed to cool off. Even if he got lost, he'd find the edge and wander along until he came across something familiar or a mage found him. They would certainly show his ass the right way home — away from them.

"It's hard to be captain." A heavy arm fell over Aaron's shoulders. Frothy beer rose in a small wave and tested the rim limits of an old, hard plastic cup. Soft plastic cups were very rare these days, though Aaron heard some families saved and washed them until they burst. Glass was still around but kept indoors, not hauled along to an End of the World gathering where a good number of them would break.

Everything in Trifecta was a finite resource. It had been for all of Aaron's life, heck for everyone here tonight.

"Paul." Aaron threw off the arm for a proper hand-tap greeting. "Thought you said we wouldn't find you at a bouncer party again."

Paul snorted into his beer.

"I figured I'd see if this was as stupid as I remember." Hoots and hollers reached them as yet another attempt failed. "Maybe even more so now." He frowned, forehead wrinkled as if trying to figure out how he'd ever had fun at one of these parties. Aaron got it. He was there.

"There's only so much to do." Paul nodded at Aaron's statement, both ruminating about the tarnished image of a once shiny thrill.

Everyone hoped to bust through. They dreamed of getting high on the shock of victory, and gaining bruises made by pavement none of them had ever touched. Eventually, people gave up, even if they visited every once in a while.

Paul, for instance, graduated four months ago. He'd gotten a job right away with the help of his dad, working on the energy systems of Trifecta. With access to outside resources cut off, Trifectans had to get creative. They'd built a semi-reliable system of water and wind turbines at the southern edge of town by using the spare parts of gasoline-powered cars and other utilities no longer operable. These provided the city with the power it needed to function. Though there was a worry about heavy equipment being so close to the school, the floodplain of the river was the flattest within human territory, and with the fewest trees, making it ideal for wind and hydropower collection.

Reclaimed chain-link solved the issue of separation. There was a running joke around how jobs were just a fence hop away after graduation. The energy department maintained and improved on the piecemeal structure, and most people hired into one of those positions.

"End of the World." The dull tone of remembrance. "So why is Brandt pissed? Coach follow through with his threats and bench him?"

"Nah, he's still in goal."

"Benefits of having your best friend's old man as coach." Paul eyed Aaron, waited to see what reaction he'd get with those words. A few years ago, sure, Aaron might have smacked beer out of Paul's grip. Talk of only being on the team because of his dad had been enough to turn the edges of his vision black with anger. Now, Aaron dipped his hand into his Trifecta letterman's jacket, one that didn't belong to him, but to whoever was captain of the squad. It used to be Paul's. This year it had become Aaron's because he'd earned it. He had nothing else to prove.

"As if my dad would let anyone play if he didn't think we could take on any outside team the very moment the barrier falls. Which, as you remember, could be any minute now, boys!"

Paul snorted and raised his glass to the memory of Coach Harwell's intensity. "I wonder how often he led the charge?" Paul pointed toward the barrier. Aaron coughed on a hard laugh.

"Probably so many times, I'm surprised he hadn't permanently dislocated his shoulder."

"Yeah," Paul laughed and struck Aaron on the back. "I'm going to grab another beer before I head out. Make sure to tuck in Brandt."

As the guy left, Aaron's stomach sunk. Without planning

the action, he caught Paul's shoulder. Paul's mouth peeked open with surprise, and Aaron almost let go, not sure why he wanted Paul to stay. He opened his mouth, searching for words, and thoughts tumbled forth.

As if his brain had been working on the problem in the background, a sudden demand for answers gripped him. What had Brandt walked away from, or walked into? Would Paul know, being older? Aaron swallowed the awkward lump in his throat and leaned in, careful to keep his voice low.

"Hey, what's the deal with the Fae?"

Paul stiffened and looked back the way he'd seen Brandt stumble with Aaron.

"Fades. Did something happen with Brandt and a Fae?"

"Not really, he just has a big mouth," Aaron hedged. "But it made me wonder. The barrier's been here for twenty years. I've heard the bogeyman stories, but the truth is we keep to ourselves."

"Man, your dad is Coach. How do you not know?"

"That's what I mean. My dad tells me how sneaky and dangerous they are, how we put them in their place right away so they didn't take what's ours. What made him feel that way? Why do we bother to… to be bothered?"

"I'm not sure," Paul admitted. "You and I are bubble born. You'd have to ask someone before us, but to be honest, the fact that the older gen doesn't talk about it should make you wary."

"What do you mean?"

"Think." Paul realized yet again his cup was empty. "Ask your dad about his high school playing days, and he'll go on for hours. Ask my Aunt Maggie about Paris, and she'll bring out every photo album she ever printed with her travels. Yet, the biggest thing in history happens — a magical wall seals our town off from the world — and no one says what happened at the beginning? You think people just figured out we were closed off and stopped trying to call or visit? Cars used to drive though Trifecta. Where is the traffic? Doesn't that stink of magic to you?"

Paul ran out of breath, the glaze on his eyes cleared on an inhale. He tried to shake a last drop from his cup. With a curse, he held it up in explanation and stepped away into the crowd as if he hadn't dumped a lifetime of doubt onto Aaron's ears.

Aaron wasn't sure how much of Paul's rant was alcohol or genuine frustration. Was it worth getting agitated over something unchangeable? Everyone was unhappy. This fading bubble had forced Fae and Witches from their home realms into this one and trapped all the races, mage or human. Still, they were peaceful, and kept out of each other's way. Aaron had as many questions with few answers, but he didn't want to end up bitter like Paul or pissed off like Brandt.

Speaking of the jerk, Aaron hopped a few times to generate heat in his chilled muscles and to pop above the other heads to check if his friend had returned. The noise level faded from raucous shouts to an indistinct murmur that suggested a lack of beer, the bounce line depleted, and people wanted to head home.

He and Brandt had arrived together, Aaron using his driving credits for a small car. Most of the time, the adults shared the thirty-two vehicles, yet they'd established a system that allowed the sixteen-year-olds their historic, coming-of-age driving tests. Now the human kids spent the week working for the privilege to borrow the city-owned cars with credits earned from community service and going to school. A few kids shared credits in order to get one of the bigger vehicles. Aaron and Brandt shared their credits because they went everywhere together. Despite the split, Aaron found he drove these days, Brandt seldom sober enough to control a vehicle.

Aaron ignored the first extinguishing of car lights as he scanned the crowd without success. Had Brandt gotten his fading self lost in the woods?

Lights stuttered out and the shadows of ancient, giant trees eclipsed the street, stopping his ability to search. Kids were getting out and slamming doors on their powerless cars, walking around them as if the answer was in the paint jobs.

"What the hell is happening?"

"They're dying."

"Didn't the fading lot attendant charge them?"

Aaron frowned, turned to his own car. His vehicle lights were on. He slid into the seat, made sure the key fob still rested in the cupholder, and pressed the engine button. With a quiet buzz the car drained, lights faded and the battery meter dropped, leaving everything at a low-glow, charge-me-now level.

Aaron banged his skull against the headrest, then bent in a belly laugh before sitting back. Even knowing he was one with the farthest walk home didn't stop him from snickering. It was only about five miles and where it wouldn't be fast, the distance was more than doable.

They'd been had, and strangely, it made him feel better.

He didn't know how she'd worked it, but Aaron had no doubt this was why the Trimarked girl had been here tonight, enacting a small bit of revenge he understood her need for, even before Brandt's idiocy. Which was funny until he realized she might have managed it with magic.

As far as anyone knew, the Trimarked Child didn't have powers, that she might not even be able to use it with a human for a mom. She'd been bound, though, on the possibility she'd be able to cast. It was possible she'd found a way around it. The thought discomforted him. He eased from his car and wondered if she could have tainted it, or if there was a film of magic he couldn't see. He wiped humid palms against his jeans.

"Aaron!" Paul shouted from a few spots toward the barrier, leaning away from a girl who hung off him and begged through crocodile tears for him to fix her car, too. Or, you know, take her home with him. "Don't worry! It will restart."

Cars along the line hummed to life. Aaron eased into the seat and turned everything off and restarted to revive his loaner. Not magic. His grip on the steering wheel tightened against the tremors. He dug deep to find the humor again and forced a chuckle.

He leaned out to thank Paul to see the guy graciously accepting his damsel's lip-lock thanks. Aaron figured she could praise him for both of them and settled in while the mayhem died down. If Brandt returned now, that would be perfect. Since he was wishing, let his friend show up renewed, rested and back to normal, just like the car.

4

EMBER

*E*mber walked twice as far as she thought the Fae could see, then she doubled back to the party, using a different path. Nicu had been rushed, which meant he was busy. She had time to locate the crew before he realized she hadn't followed orders. Anyway, he could shove it. Nicu didn't have to bargain for food like she did, and since he was keeping his involvement to barking commands, Ember continued to need Chase.

The game trail she'd chosen led toward the barrier, a bit wide of a straight shot to the End of the World. One of the more remote spots in Trifecta, this area was a favorite of hers. She slowed out of habit. Full of ancient trees almost as large in diameter as her entire house, the pines stood as guards of peace. Unbothered by the Redwoods, bits of mountain poked through the needled forest floor in sheets, bumps, and boulders broad enough to have become yet another place for a tree to take root. Human territory, it was too far from the civilized streets of Town for the humans to visit regularly, and it was often all hers. Here she sometimes found proof that the boundary was selectively penetrable whenever a blue jay flitted through or a black squirrel dashed across. Once, she saw a tawny deer use the very path she tread. It soared through in a graceful leap, a passage no person could hope to make on their own.

Not tonight, though. The sounds of the party would keep the wildlife away. The bass drifted through the trees, distant music punctured the silence along with the sudden roar and fade of the crowd as another idiot slammed against the barrier and gained bruises on purpose. That was her destination. A heavy shiver urged her forward despite a deep reluctance.

Raucous feet crunched dead leaves and snapped an old dry branch. A human, since the mages never made so much noise. Ember picked up her pace, sure it was Chase or one of the other members of his crew and eager to find out if they finished and were ready to put an end to tonight's deal.

The drunken utterance came too late to alert her it wasn't someone expected. She skidded to a stop two feet from Brandt and his black eye.

"Bitch." More sober than at their last meeting, he captured her with renewed speed and strength. His fingers grabbed a thick chunk at the front of her sweater. Her surprise had kept her from backing up, but remaining frozen would be a mistake. She allowed him to pull her in, controlled the momentum to spin them around and get him off balance, just enough to make sure he applied his free arm for stability rather than land a punch. She didn't want to knock him over yet, not when his grip might take her with him.

"I thought you were looking for me?" Ember asked.

"Why in convergence do you think that?"

Good, she'd surprised him into conversation. Ember shrugged and lay her hands over the fist still locked in her outermost hoodie. Both his thick brows raised when she took a voluntary step closer.

"It's okay. It happens."

"Are you crazy?"

"I get it. Curiosity can be too much."

"Wha—"

"Sometimes a human gets curious about what it's like to be with a non-human. Even one like me."

Brandt's jaw dropped. He snatched his hand away. Ember put distance between them while keeping him squared up, tugged the bottom of her hoodie to smooth where he'd bunched it, and watched for a path of escape.

Drunk or not, it didn't take Brandt long to realize she'd tricked him. He rushed her. Quick goalie reflexes helped him grip her right bicep and shoved her into the barrier. His free forearm crossed over her neck, cut off her oxygen, pressed her head into the transparent surface behind her, an illusion of freedom as impenetrable as a brick wall.

"Where is your crazy pixie, now?"

Ember closed her eyes, refused to let the lack of air distract her from what she had to do. She tapped her fingers against the barrier, made sure blood flowed despite her captivity. Tap tap tap against the captive power faster than she'd ever done, with more need than she'd ever had.

Tiny vibrations echoed from her fingertips. Brandt pushed harder. She gagged against the pressure, choked again on an inhale of his alcohol saturated breath. Another bite of static electricity nipped as she worked the energy, something she hadn't felt before, but she'd never tried this so fast and it was hard to worry when sensation drained from her hands. Had to act now.

Her left palm slammed into the barrier. Brandt laughed at what he assumed was an attempt to breathe. He didn't see the pulses grow, or notice the hole when her elbow felt the sheet of energy shift. She punched his ribs, pulled on his arm, and forced him to turn and spin, then his hands to windmill in order to keep to his feet while he took one step back, then two.

The ripples only she could see stiffened and solidified into a solid slab. The small opening she'd compelled into existence was now closed.

When Brandt reached for her again. His fist slammed into the barrier from the outside with such fierce intensity she heard the crack of knuckles. His scream caught deep in the woods, masked by the shouts of the party goers and the thud of their music. He fell to his knees, eyes wide as he looked up at her now and realized what she had done.

She had thrown Brandt out of Trifecta.

Ember coughed and returned oxygen to starved cells, her palm flat against the restored, solid barrier. Gratefulness flooded her mind and left her floating, her body trembling with harsh little jerks. She'd been so afraid she wouldn't get the pattern out in time, that Brandt wouldn't land in the tiny space she'd be able to open, or make it through before it closed. She'd done it, though, and now she was safe.

Another crunch of leaves stopped her heart, her breath forgotten.

Not safe.

Who had seen her? Who was going to see Brandt?

"Well, I guess no rescue is necessary."

Blood and air rushed to Ember's brain with such force she swayed on her feet, her vision blackened.

"Whoa, there," Chase murmured, one of his hands at her elbow, another holding a flashlight with a bag slung over the same shoulder. She leaned into his lanky frame, gripped the smooth fabric of his tunic hoodie, cut long and narrow. Her knees locked because she refused to lean too far into his grip and absolutely did not want to fall. It only took a moment before Ember nodded and Chase removed his small bit of support.

"Don't worry. Kevin's got him." Chase gestured with a sharp thrust of his chin that flicked shoulder length hair against a hollowed cheek.

"What?" Ember looked out with the help of Chase's light. Kevin was one of Chase's spies on the outside, someone she'd sent through years ago. He and a few others gripped Brandt, keeping him from running back to the road where he would have been able to tell the party goers what happened.

Verge, what a mess. She owed Chase again, but for the promise of safety, she'd pay.

"Don't worry too much about it." Chase's reassurance sounded more like approval. Fantastic. Ember burned with fatigue from head to the hole-filled soles of her shoes. "That's what friends are for."

Ember huffed, watched him from the corner of her eye. "I didn't realize our agreement extended to friendship."

"Think about it. The way tonight played out for you — how many fights did you get into? — a few friends might be beneficial."

And what would that cost me?

"Do you have my food?"

Chase's attention shifted from the gang of adolescent men free of the barrier. As usual he gave nothing away, no sign if he wanted to be on that side or this, or if he decided she wasn't worth the risk to help anymore, balance sheet or no. He thumbed the shoulder strap of the messenger bag, her payment for the evening.

The food inside the tote might be from the small backyard gardens the humans maintained, or the Witches' farms along the river, or Fae hunters that supplemented meat where the human efforts failed. Ember didn't care, was fine with keeping her debt in Chase's fair hands as opposed to others. Mostly, she just wanted to eat.

"It's a heavy one. Do you need help to get it home?"

Ember answered by holding out her hand.

"Sure?" Chase asked. "There's a Fae guarding your door. Come with us to watch the humans freak over their cars and I'll drop you after."

Ember didn't move. Chase flung the bag from his shoulder to hers, then stepped close. One finger to her chin, he tilted her face up and tsked.

"Next time, throw them out before they hurt you."

Ember jerked away from his touch and slipped passed, tired of being stuck between a guy and the barrier.

"Use the tunnels to avoid her."

The words weren't a suggestion. Ember would have taken that route without them. Chase meant to remind her of another favor he'd completed for her, clearing the underground halls that led to the old maintenance building she and her mom now called home. She realized with a grim set to her mouth that he would not give her a pass. Chase would keep her secrets and call in her debt.

A problem for a different day.

Ember rounded a corner of the game trail and hiked the heavy bag further up her shoulder when it slipped. The motion took her attention for only a second, plenty of time for Edan to appear on the path, his movement unnoticed, lounging on a tree as if he'd been waiting for a while.

Ember swung a defensive step backward, gripped the strap against her body. She dared to look over the trail, calculated the distance between where they stopped and where she'd talked with Chase.

Edan couldn't know.

Ember turned her attention to the Fae. Her empty stomach clenched. She stood firm, forced her eyes to focus on the threat.

She was forbidden from using magic. The mages expected she would wield an uncontrollable energy, a time bomb that had the ability to set worlds on fire, should it manifest. Or, at least, that was what they said to justify keeping her segregated and vilified. Ember didn't know for sure, hoped to never find out. It didn't matter.

The mages expected Fae or Witch magic from her. Neither described how she manipulated the barrier. She didn't pull atoms of magic from physical things, or use the flow of it to force her intentions. She knocked, and the hardened magic parted, though not for long. Gaps always closed within seconds, so it wasn't like she could line everyone up and wave them through en masse. She didn't know how often the trick was possible and had no plan to become a public servant only to die from overexertion. Some people might remain stuck, anyway. She had never stepped outside. The bubble continued to block her despite her skill. The irony of having the capability without the ability to take advantage of it left a sour taste.

Even without Fae or Witch influence, though, she still Worked magic. Even if she considered this talent more of a party trick than helpful, albeit one no one else had mastered, it was a trick that would be viewed as the gateway into a more twisted, forbidden power. The knowledge that she held some brand of power would be all the confirmation they needed: She would become a threat big enough to eliminate.

That's all it took. Edan seeing her Work on the barrier. Edan alerting his Elders. The Elders telling the human council, and the humans didn't care as long as they had their illusion of equality. The Fae could pass judgement on someone no one claimed as one of their kind. She'd belong to them.

Edan shifted from the tree, angled one moment and stood straight the next. Measured strides eased through the space between them. Ember studied the lines of his tailored coat and pressed slacks meant to be elegant while ready for a run. He lacked a bulge that might hide a weapon, not even under his knitted hat, and she tried to find solace with his empty palms.

No concern for personal distance, Edan imposed upon her. His chest emanated a rich earth scent that thickened in her throat before the moment those bare hands reached her neck.

Fingers wrapped to meet over her tattoo, thumbs pressured the corners of her jaw to force exposure. Pained muscles pulled taut, the strain echoed in her wrinkled brow. Ember's involuntary swallow increased discomfort, compounded by Edan's study of the evidence from Brandt's attack.

He knew.

Tears clawed at her dry eyes as he leaned into her and his heated breath mingled with the autumn chill to leave a cloying mist against her skin.

"Be grateful I am the one who saw, and not Nicu," he whispered. "Be thankful for the circumstances that protect you."

Ember struggled against the loss of strength and a flush of vertigo. He hadn't killed her.

"Wh-what circumstances?"

"Don't fall off."

Translation, see you soon.

Edan filtered back into the shadows and left her to deal with her own shattered sense of security. She knew better than to think he didn't watch her.

Oh. Verge. Owing Edan, a Fae. It might be easier to be dead.

With a slow scrape, the strap of her bag eased across her shoulder, then sunk with a thud. The pressure didn't register at first, though the pain filtered into her peripheral thoughts. Why did her foot hurt?

Oh, food. Food to take home.

She had to get home.

Ember hoisted the load with both hands and cradled it in front of her body without bothering with the strap. She ran, careless of the jostle her quick movements caused to the contents.

Circumstances saved her. Whatever that meant. Only, she wasn't convinced keeping her life meant she'd been saved.

5

NICU

*S*ticky wet coated Nicu's skin, and tickled the points of his elbows as it dripped to darken the concrete. The early morning chill hadn't been enough to stop his body from generating heat while he'd moved through a functional strength circuit. Battle ropes, climbing walls, balance posts and pieces of tree trunk almost as long as his arm span littered the large clearing that had once been a picnic pavilion.

At the finish, he fell into a simple pull-up pattern. Pull, pike, lengthen, lower. Pull, pike, lengthen, lower. He didn't count, instead he remained mindful during each motion of muscle with bone, the flex of skin over flesh, how the white cloth of his tank tried to contain each movement. Tremors suggested this was the last one. He was running out of energy. And he went again.

His fingers became slick against the metal bar and threatened his control. With a scowl, he eased himself into full arm extension, then dropped three feet to the ground, knees bent to cushion impact.

A slow clap guided his attention to the side of the ring where Daz leaned against a pillar fitted for barehanded climbing. Though both Fae dressed in baggy joggers to counter the morning frost, Daz still wore his loose sweater and it was clean of sweat marks, evidence of his fresh arrival. He wasn't the only one. The training space had been empty when Nicu began with false dawn, but now the sun was full over the horizon and others had filled in while he'd meditated over his reps.

The newcomers were scouts or hunters, all Terraborn. Born to the energies of this realm, they were more in tune with the forest and more willing to explore in the name of running patrols. In contrast to the human's pastime of banging their heads against a wall, young Fae trained.

Never off duty, training in the mornings was the closest he came to having time off. Nicu found solace in the repetitions, pride with increased strength, and a deep satisfaction knowing he was only responsible for his own fitness, no one else's. His hours here almost appeared like freedom. The other Terraborn were well aware this was the place to approach him, as evident with Daz's morning greeting.

"I was heading to the sparring mats but saw your beautiful form," Daz said. "Working off some frustration, Nix?"

"Yeah," Nicu grabbed the towel he'd thrown at the base of the pull-up bar. He studied the horizon as he wiped off. The day was still new. He had time. "The mats, huh? Care for a match?"

Daz tilted his head. "How long have you been training?"

"I'm not sure. An hour on the course."

"Then verge, no," Daz laughed. "Not when you're blowing off steam." Nicu took the ribbing with a shallow, upward tilt of a smile.

"Five point lead?"

Daz debated for a moment, then shrugged.

"Nah. You have time for something else, though?"

"What are you thinking?"

"A chat. Back at the shop?"

"You just got here."

"I need motivation. I have a lot of work to complete before

I train today." Daz looked between Nicu and the next closest Fae, as close to fidgeting as Nicu had seen him. "If you're busy…"

"It's fine. Let's go." They left the training grounds after Nicu dropped his towel in a collection basket, pulled on a wide necked sweater he'd brought with him, then headed into the heart of Center.

The humans who last camped in these cottages would not recognize the redesigned buildings. When the Fae arrived, the log cabins had been solid, though weathered from disuse. A decade or more of fallen leaves from old, imported maple trees had been left to rot over the soil. The twenty original structures had not offered enough space. The Fae wanted the location, anyway, though it had taken a while before they'd started improvements.

During the Fade, the Witches spent their time learning the ways of Terra, and initiated meetings to discuss their new situation. After many sessions, the leaders of each group drafted the Laws of Convergence. The Fae cared little about an agreement they believed temporary. The Fae were not willing to admit defeat. They refused to acclimate, confident magic would return them home.

It did not.

The arrangement left the Fae with the campground and bound to Laws of Convergence so simple that their ancestors would feel shame if they knew Fae had helped shape them. Yet, the rules of war and peace were clear, and they had come out with the most important win, the territory within Trifecta that held a faint energy overlay to their own realm.

The learning curve had lasted years after the final Fade. They had a more difficult time adjusting from their reddish sky to the brilliant blue of Terra. The particles of magic they pulled from the atoms that built every living thing on Gypsum were more slippery within Terra and more ingrained in the material they were part of. As months passed, the Fae accepted this move may not be temporary, and they needed to regain the strength that belonged to their race.

Once they learned how to manage the more stubborn power of the Terran realm, they shaped Center for comfort. Builders and artists, the Fae created masterpieces of wood and vine and earth. Luxury living quarters were built underground. The upper cabins were renovated to service the community and offer a very limited view of Fae culture should outsiders ever visit them.

Daz apprenticed out of the cabin that had become the weaver's shop. The modest storefront opened to the courtyard, an intermediate door led to where the actual weaving took place. Multiple looms lined up in rows. Closer to the rear entrance, long pine tables sat empty, waiting for Fae to sort gathered materials to be Worked. Novices started with plant parts, then graduated to yarn Work, and on to finer cloth making. Daz's table was covered in wide-blade grasses and small, brown vines.

"How fast can you copy a spell?" Daz asked, organizing the scattered supplies of his workstation to clear space. He pulled a completed bowl and a few more just begun from storage shelves underneath the tabletop.

"Daz, I cannot." Nicu ran a fingertip along one of the partially woven green reeds.

If magic were a pond, Nicu's hands would come up dry if he dipped them in, where another Fae's fingers filled with possibility defined by the will of the magic gathered. Skilled crafters meditated with their medium, felt through its essential form, and found the lines that allowed ease of movement. The craftsman used methods intended to work alongside, not against, the natural patterns of the world. Wood shed its layers to reveal the curves and dips of nymphs, rushing rivers and flowering vines. Raw fibers spun into delicate threads that bent and wove into rich cloth. Stone chipped away into fine dust for paints and brick, producing polished surfaces that revealed expressive faces. But never for Nicu.

"You can't create on your own, I know," Daz rushed. "But I've been thinking - because I'm so behind and I'm desperate. What if I gave you the pattern of my magic to follow?"

Nicu grounded himself and took a deep breath to find balance. His contact with the reed shifted as skin sought the energies. Magic thread through every stiff fiber. He saw where they settled into place. With his free hand, he reached for the completed bowl to compare the two. Focused on the unfinished piece, he found the magical particles Daz had gathered from the materials.

A soft grunt of effort and Nicu had that power beholden to his own will. The invisible force was tangible to his inner senses, perceived rather than seen. Magic was difficult to find, collect, and hold on to. Fae were taught from birth until extracting the energy became second nature, first in recognizing, then from experimenting. Mentors gave small tasks that increased in difficulty, so by the time Fae reached ten years, they'd become as familiar with the feel and use of magic as they were with clothing and feeding themselves.

He gleaned Daz's pattern of magic placed within the structure of the woven plants. He twisted the pooled power based on the finished bowl's design and watched as the reeds wove around each other, curved up, then over into form. Daz rushed forward to collect more magic. Nicu encouraged the plant fibers to shift their color and pulled tints and shades until the pattern matched.

Nicu let go, and the bowl fell apart.

"Verge." Daz's disappointment echoed the collapse.

"An interesting experiment." Nicu controlled his own dissatisfaction with a roll of his shoulders.

"The master weavers keep saying there are no shortcuts. I hate it when they're right." Daz's smile lacked energy. "I guess I can't get out of this one. Thanks for trying."

Nicu nodded in affirmation.

"Duty calls, it seems," Daz said.

"I'll leave you to it."

"No, I mean, for you." Daz gestured to the front entrance where Branna stood in the doorway, dressed in black, mummy-wrap fleece leggings. A shirt with cutouts along the length of her arm allowed a glimpse of her scythe-shaped tattoos, her thumbs hooked through holes in the cuffs. Glossy hair smoothed up her scalp until it crowned into a puffy bun, her preferred style.

Nicu stepped out of the shop, looked up to find the courtyard busy with Fae beginning the day, but not so focused they didn't notice the Child's guardian and his mate.

With attention fixated on them, Nicu pressed his cheek to Branna's in greeting. Years ago the council declared their lives joined, an ancient practice rarely enacted, one that suggested marriage but did not enforce it. The Elder Council thought it kind to restrict their choices. As the only two tainted Fae, no other Fae would have them, Terraborn or not.

Both present at the Trimarked Child's birth, both had come out mutated after a High Magic spell to end the threat rebounded and ricocheted, leaving death and resurrection and altered powers in its wake. Nicu could not gather raw magic, and as he'd learned with Daz, to shape something physical with it, either.

Nicu needed a spell of the intangible. Like a parasite, he claimed the thickened ropes of power and twisted them to his desire, even one outside their preferred shape. A spell cast to cool the inside of a building might twist into a city-wide storm with his command. A Work meant to locate a lost item could be reshaped into a campfire.

The ability to manipulate and change tied him to the barrier, a power created by a mutation of the Veil. The Veil had been a gossamer shield between realms, something Fae could pass through as easily as parting a curtain when they willed it.

Now, the magic had hardened, bubbled, a wall of glass unbreakable by every force the Fae and Witches had tried.

Branna was the victim of a darker mutation, one born along with her own rebirth upon a miraculous resurrection. Her chosen color was a reminder to herself and a challenge to the Fae to remember who she was, that her power stood unique among them. Not touched by High Magic, but by the cost of it. Death. Necromancy.

Their curse became the Fae's gain. Instead of having to assign a pure Fae to the Trimarked Child, they assigned those already tarnished by chaos, a shield to protect the uncorrupted. Bonding the tainted Fae together within responsibilities and as mates left Nicu and Branna unable to connect with the pure Fae, another level of protection.

If the Child proved dangerous, a more powerful Fae would offer their skills. Not a moment before. So Nicu maintained that distance, interpreted his orders to mean the Child had to become a genuine danger, not simply a nuisance. Her chaotic choices might inspire another Fae to interpret her as worthy of removal, but Nicu knew otherwise. This realm birthed chaos, and Ember was part of that. Nothing she had done posed a risk great enough for Fae sacrifice. Nicu would approach the council only if the Child was no longer in control.

Nicu rose from his bow and noticed the tight features and the slight compression of Branna's lips. She did not share his view regarding his duty between the Fae and the Trimarked Child and considered his definition too broad. They refrained from speaking of it to keep the peace, so it was with only a small twist of trepidation that Nicu posed his question.

"What has encouraged your ire?"

A twitch of her fingers and a flash of her angry mauve eyes gave her wordless answer. Something he'd done, and large enough that she did not want to speak with witnesses. They were going for a run, then. Nicu's wave to Daz went unseen, the Fae focused on work.

"Good morning!" someone called over the polished cobbles. Nicu and Branna ignored the greeting, knowing it wasn't for them. They overlooked the intended recipient who looked up from his work to accept the pleasantry, only to blanch at their approach.

"Did I forget to leave my specter at home?" Branna's quiet words leached her compounded irritation. A nearby Fae heard her tone and rushed away from the building column he carved.

"You could get it a leash," Edan said. He fell in beside them, and the atmosphere in the courtyard shifted toward calm. As the only untainted Terraborn of their group, Edan brought a sense of normalcy to the unit and tolerance among the Fae increased, then turned to relief as the three passed.

The balm did not reach Branna. They were not far into the upwardly steep path of their woodland jog before her strain snapped.

"Were you aware the Child had not gone straight home?" The words reverberated around them.

"No."

Branna's mouth clicked shut when presented with Nicu's brief, honest answer. She stomped out a few strides.

"Edan said the Ternate has risen."

"Yes," Nicu said.

A few more loud footfalls expressed Branna's displeasure, but it wasn't long before she re-established patience along with silent steps.

"This may compound the issue." Her dark eyes studied the tree branches. So she'd hoped for a bigger fight to buffer her own news. "Something is chipping away at the barrier."

It took Nicu every force of will to keep his body in rhythm against the consistent incline. Could this be Ember? If it was ... He weighed his fealty to the Fae against his duty to the Child for half a heartbeat before putting the question aside. If the hybrid girl caused this, he would debate plans. Nothing could be done until he was certain of the cause. "How did you discover this?"

"I noticed the spirits' luminescence reflected off pieces of Veil energy last night, glitter dispersed across the landscape. It wasn't much, barely sufficient to catch my attention."

"What does that mean?" Edan asked. Nicu opened his mouth for a deep breath, the action meant to hide the tension in his lips.

"I don't know," Branna huffed. "Someone's trying to get out of Trifecta, or break in? They're tiny fragments, maybe large enough for a thought."

Nicu rolled his shoulders with the news. The scatter could also be a sign of movement. Last night's wave wasn't the first one, but it produced the most violent reaction.

A layer of cold perspiration pricked under the damp caused by exercise. Connected to the barrier, he'd investigated the waves when they'd begun. Clues at the outskirts of human territory and an investigation into who used the area had led him toward Ember. He refocused on potential damage to the Veil's power. Once he recognized the events as nonthreatening, he had stopped gathering intel.

Because he'd once granted Ember a promise. All Fae had the ability to grant promises, agreements enhanced and enforced by High Magic. These covenants were the basis of much of the humans' fairy lore and were a way for Fae to engage High Magic on another's behalf without invoking it themselves. As a young Fae, Nicu had thought this side-step an ingenious way to secure his success with his Fae and Trimarked duties. Instead, it had become another burden, and just as powerful as his blood ties to the Fae.

"Can you identify if this phenomenon is external or internal?" Nicu asked as they rounded a bend that would lead them downhill. There were too many variables within these events for him to assume a cause for Branna's discovery. Wist's external experimenter was a likely culprit. Leaping to a conclusion would tilt the balance he fought to maintain.

Branna mimicked his answers. "No."

"Wist suggested someone tampered with the barrier," Edan spoke with intention, echoing Nicu's earlier thought.

"Ember's house is just off the center of Trifecta." Branna shook her head. "It could be something different."

"It could be," Edan agreed. "Yet, though Ember's home is far from the border, it is near No Man's Land."

Nicu stopped at the bottom of a decline before the mountain rose one last time, then descended the rest of the way to Center. His ability to hide the depth of his agitation cracked, and he turned away, though the wide trees and rocky terrain left little option beyond staying on the path. Three deep breaths returned enough control to allow him to face his companions.

"Do you have more to share?"

Branna shrugged, gestured with an empty palm.

Edan linked his hands behind his back, spread his legs and met Nicu's demand with silence. Edan was, in part, a spy for the Fae. The only pure Terraborn of the group, he was a vigorous collector of information and the Fae expected him to share. As far as Nicu had seen, Edan preferred to keep most secrets close, both a boon and a frustration.

Nicu's trust in him was situational. Sending Edan last night might prove a mistake, though at the moment there was no sign he knew anything relevant. It would be redundant to point out Edan was keeping something from Nicu. He hoped, as always, that whatever secrets Edan collected did not prove dangerous.

"This information is not unimportant," Nicu ground out. "The Chaos Star has risen. Wist has informed us someone is trying to press in from outside Trifecta. Now you find fragments of Veil material around the hybrid's house. We cannot risk losing control over this. It threatens peace. It threatens lives. We need to gather adequate intelligence so we can react correctly and not be blindsided as we had been with the convergence. Edan, I need to know what your contacts say. Make sure it's done. Today."

Edan's features closed in response to Nicu's mention of sources beyond the borders. A twitch in his jaw was the only hint the other Fae felt uncomfortable, and a twist to his mouth as if he disclosed something bitter.

"There has been a problem with communication."

New knowledge. Nicu took a deep breath to ward off the sharp pain reverberating between his temples. A quick scan of Edan's discomfort showed him it was not the secret he kept most close.

"Is there a way to restore it?"

Edan's hesitation allowed the natural noise of the forest to drift between them. He stepped closer. "I have an option. I'm not sure it's viable or what it may cost." Words unsaid, not Fae approved.

"Then explore with caution," Nicu murmured.

Edan's brisk nod acknowledged he'd heard. Nicu studied him a moment longer, then turned to Branna. "Try to discover if these remnants are elsewhere in Trifecta, or solely around the Child's house before we concentrate on No Man's Land. I will check for activity there after I assess the health of the barrier itself."

The pair left him on the path, their direction toward Center. What he had not pointed out, what he could not say, was this was a direct threat to the Trimarked Child. Nicu needed both Edan and Branna to support his balance between duty and was glad they were his team. However, there were too many secrets, too much expectation between them to forge true trust.

Branna would want to address the Elders, if only to end her babysitting responsibilities. Edan would, perhaps, be forced to share secrets even Nicu did not know he had, things best kept unspoken. At this point, it was unnecessary to include the Elders. Nicu was strong in body and spirit. He had worked his entire life to manage control within himself, to use that knowledge to help control her. He was not as quick as Branna or his Elders to assume Ember's chaos would break the realms further than they were, and had seen no proof she was capable of such a thing, despite her reckless choices.

His caution now proved justified. Today came with sharp awareness that the hybrid girl's chaos might not be the only he had to fight. He did not appreciate realizing he was unprepared.

Nicu practiced patience as his team dropped behind the next hill, and he was surrounded by solitude. With a pivot, Nicu faced the closest tree, swung a stiff right hook, dented his knuckles against pitted bark, jarred his shoulder, the sound compact and short lived in the thick wood.

6

AARON

*T*hree miles into a five-mile run, Aaron sagged with the unfamiliar weight of defeat. In search of Brandt, he'd run the asphalt roads, passed homes that faced downhill toward the neighbor's backyard, space so thick with young pines and owner-planted maple or birch trees that they blocked the view of the house on the next street. He looped along the grid of colonial and saltbox houses, past Brandt's house to find it silent. Other team members' homes were still dark in the early Saturday hours. Brandt wasn't somewhere on the open school grounds where he sometimes crashed when he didn't want to deal with his dad's temper.

The skin on Aaron's back itched with discomfort. He weighed knocking on Brandt's door as he jogged toward home, but decided against it. Brandt and his dad fought like wet cats, and starting one of their famous shouting matches was not Aaron's first inclination. His friend would turn up. He always did.

Then again, Brandt hadn't challenged a Fae before. Aaron tugged at the front of his sweat-soaked shirt. Damn.

Had he found real trouble in this stupidly quiet town? Had he gone after Nicu?

Aaron reached the uppermost street and slowed his jog to a walk, taking this last stretch to cool down. He pulled air in through his nose, careful to keep it measured so the chill didn't cramp his hot lungs. He stared at his house with trepidation, as if the structure reflected his dad and might tell him through shaded windows or painted columns what mood the old man was in this morning.

Aaron stretched against the stairs of the front porch, a delaying tactic that left him without answers and more cold than cooled down.

He strode through the front door into the entryway. Straight ahead, stairs rose to the second floor. Left took him around to his dad's study and the living room. To his right sat a long, empty table they only used when members of the team came over for dinner.

"Dad?"

His shout reached every part of the two-story home. Yelling proved the most efficient system for finding each other. Brandt had always joined right in, claiming it was the bachelor's chosen form of communication, which made Aaron wonder if things would be different if his mom hadn't died when he was two. With or without her, loud shouts and long workouts had become the language of their small family. For proof, a gruff sound greeted him, muffled by layers of house that told him his dad was in their basement gym.

Aaron passed through the dining room into the kitchen, which was a mess with dirty dishes in the sink, a used blender on the brown granite island and binders full of coaching papers spread out. The basement door hung wide open and he lobbed down stairs stacked under the upstairs set. Gus warmed up with light bench presses.

"Good, you can spot me." Gus loaded more weights. Aaron noted the plates and mirrored them on the opposite side. "Did you get the car back?"

"Yeah, last night."

Gus grunted as he rolled his spine onto the bench, then shifted until he aligned himself. His wide leg shorts drooped halfway to the floor, workout clothes the only kind Gus cared to buy from the Witches. Otherwise, it was human hand-me-downs and repairs for Aaron and him, which was basically the wardrobe of all Trifectan humans, though each one had their own preference for new, clean-cloth items.

Aaron settled into a steady stance at his dad's head, hands out and ready to spot. Gus put the weights down after eight reps and shook his arms out.

"Did any of you idiots break through last night?"

"Oh, yeah," Aaron said. "The pop heard around the world."

Gus chuckled before he sipped from his water bottle.

"Back in my day, there was barely enough room for us to fit between the trees. Fewer kids these days, I guess," Gus mumbled, referring to the low population bust with a frown. Locked up tight, many people didn't want to add kids to this trap, but that wasn't what he wanted to discuss.

Aaron hesitated and checked the clock. His dad would go for another set soon.

"So, um." Aaron bounced, fingers rested on the silver bar. Gus twisted and looked at him with a raised brow. "We talk a lot about how the mages are assholes and such, but uh, could you tell me what they did? At the beginning?"

"What the hell kind of question is that?"

Aaron winced against the echo bouncing off concrete and mirrors, set his feet and slid his hands toward the bar as if spotting already, a concession of sorts for pissing off his dad.

"Last night, there were some guys saying they could take the Fae," Nothing like the I-have-a-friend strategy. "Nothing's happened in twenty years, they think, so what's up with them, anyway? I wasn't sure what to say. Not sure if it was possible. Taking a Fae. I just thought, you know, that you would know."

The added ego boost worked to calm his dad. Instead of

boiling over, he sat there at a simmer, face reddened but shoulders relaxed.

"Their arrival messed everything up," Gus said. "We weren't rich, but we had it good. State champions of soccer. Not too bad at football, either. Good."

"Yeah, the glass factory closed, right? Brandt's dad worked there." Aaron hoped to move the conversation along by skimming over it himself. "The barrier stopped us from getting materials and we couldn't send anything out, so—"

"It wasn't only things, Aaron." Gus licked his lips and checked the time. "Let me get these out."

Eight more reps, during which Aaron had to focus on the movement. His dad had fake dropped the bar before to make sure Aaron was alert. Gus appeared too preoccupied for that test today. He sat back up and grabbed a towel to mop his face and neck.

"Take a Fae. Yeah, pretty confident you could do that. I could do that. Fist to fist, they aren't that much different from us. We're as matched as anyone else who works out the same. But they have magic."

"But... they haven't used it against us?"

Gus watched the second hand tick in its circle. Usually he took active rests between sets, skipping or jumping jacks, but Aaron figured his heart rate raced from the effort of their conversation, negating the need.

"This goes back to the Fade. It happened in the three years prior to convergence. No one understood what was happening. The Fae seemed fine enough, a bit confused and... dizzy. The Witches were quick to light an ass on fire if a person tried to start something. It was a strange thing. They'd be here, we'd remember. They'd leave, we'd forget. When they returned it wasn't new again, it wasn't amnesia, it was just... We didn't remember."

"That's not so complicated. Why doesn't anyone talk about it?"

Gus sighed. "Look. The barrier locked everyone in place. No one could fix it. There was some fighting, then the Laws were hashed out. We decided to let you kids be kids and keep the pointless parts out of it."

Aaron gripped the bar and twisted. "So what happened?"

"What?"

"What did the Fae actually do?"

Gus darkened from within, blood thickened in his neck.

"They are the ones who kept making us forget. I can't tell you how I know, it's a gut thing. And when I think about it, if I focus really hard, I'm pretty sure they're still doing it."

Aaron wrinkled his brow, not understanding what his dad was trying to explain.

"What do you mean? We don't forget them."

"Really? How many times a day do you think about your school teachers? Brandt? The team? And now many times a day do you think of mages, either the Fae or Witch kind?"

Aaron shrugged. "They're not part of my every day. The other people are."

Gus slapped the towel against his thigh. His scowl made it clear he wasn't sure how to explain how he felt any better than he just had.

"I suppose it doesn't matter. Fact is, the type of magic they do goes beyond growing flowers or lighting people on fire, and I'm more pissed about the magic I can't see." Gus frowned at the floor. "Why are you asking these questions again?"

"Brandt wants to fight a Fae." The truth was a risk, but one that might get his dad to focus.

Gus dropped his head, hands dangled between spread knees. "His father will kill him."

"Not if he did it," Aaron said.

"Yeah, Karl hates the mages. Everything he had was tied up in those glass factories, but he's not stupid."

Gus pressed out his last set, grunted at the end, and

collapsed with a clang onto the hooks. When he sat up, Aaron disassembled the bar.

"How much did you run today?"

"Five miles."

"Do ten tomorrow. One of you knuckleheads will break through that barrier one of these days. I bet we take State back first try." Gus stood, the towel twisted between his hands. "And, hey. Brandt will forget this. Or you'll tell him to. And if he doesn't, he can start running with you, school day or not. It's time to get that kid's mind on something other than booze."

An excellent plan, Aaron thought as he headed upstairs for a shower, if he ever found Brandt.

If Brandt wasn't in the human part of Trifecta, that left the mage neighborhoods. There was a decent chance drunk Brandt tried to find Center, just a few miles north from the party spot. Of course, he didn't know how to get there. Brandt might be lost. Or worse, caught.

Would the Fae jail a human? Aaron wasn't sure his dad had an answer for that one, and if Gus learned Brandt was missing, he'd go straight to Karl. Aaron had run interference between Brandt, Karl, and the world for so long, he wasn't ready to give up, yet.

Showered and dressed for the day, Aaron made some space at the island where he sat on a round, wood stool. He swallowed a bowl of oatmeal and a few hard boiled eggs while he tried to figure out what to do next. His best bet would be to track down Nicu, then confront the Fae most likely to have something to do with Brandt's disappearance. How to do that?

The Trimarked girl.

She didn't live far from him. The paved street continued three houses down. After that, it turned to gravel for a few yards before a gate blocked where the forest had overtaken the road that had once led to the campground.

In the space between the last colonial house and the gate, a concrete structure that had been a part of the old flooding system perched up on the hill. Ember's mom, Susan Lee, converted it into a home years ago.

The whole of Trifecta knew Nicu guarded the Trimarked on behalf of the Fae. Their run-in last night proved it.

Strength to strength, his dad said.

Aaron pushed away from the island and ran out the front door. Fist to fist sounded like an even enough match up if it meant he found his friend.

7

EMBER

*E*mber cowered on her low mattress, saturated in the darkness of her windowless room. Breath gasped into her body, rattled back out. Holy fades. Her forehead dropped, only fingers locked into the length of her hair kept her head from falling to the floor at her feet. She'd slept in winks, listened to each breeze and tree branch creak, always on the verge of losing her battle with fear.

Would Edan keep his word? Had he promised not to say anything? Were the Fae coming to get her, to test her, to lock her up if they found out their binding magic hadn't been enough?

Sure, Chase knew, and even helped her out sometimes. He offered nothing for free, but the cost was always one she could afford.

She could not afford to owe a Fae. She could not trust Edan. Ember blew warm breath between trembling fingers, tried to find heat and a solution.

Her only contact with the Fae was with Nicu. If she found trouble, he appeared. She pissed him off with minimal effort, which was only fair after his constant reminders to keep to herself. Then again, if she'd listened to him — it didn't matter. She needed to ask someone for help.

Ember pulled the chain connected to the single, naked lightbulb stuck into her closet-slash-bedroom ceiling. She grabbed her pillow, a bunched up sweater, and threw it on over the slept-in waffle henley. The open clothes rack that lined the wall opposite her bed provided a thicker, larger hoodie to zip on top. A candy wrapper in the bottom of her shoe blocked the holes worn through the soles to keep her feet dry and it wouldn't slip as long as she tied the laces tight enough. The shoes still fit, so she didn't want to trade for new ones, yet.

Her closet opened to an unobstructed view of the front door, which boasted their only window. No light came through the panes. Too dark to head out.

Ember peeked around the ancient sofa sleeper that no longer folded into a couch. Her mom laid on pillows and watched the always-on-TV, tuned to the single channel Trifecta broadcasted. Children's cartoons. Early morning, just not sunrise.

"Hungry?" she asked her mom.

Susan hummed in answer. Ember skirted their bistro size dining set to grab a pot off the stove and filled it from their only sink, part of their two piece bathroom opposite her closet. Water boiling, she reached into one of their three lower cupboards and grabbed a brand new container of quick oats brought in with last night's haul. Another cabinet held bowls and spoons.

"Leave the oven on?"

Ember blinked in slow acceptance. "Of course." Now she understood why Susan stayed under the blanket. "I'll hang the wall quilts soon."

Electricity came free with their location, a forgotten city-powered utility building. The furnace, however, hadn't worked for as long as they'd lived here and they'd found alternatives for staying warm. Though hanging the blankets took from the layers of Ember's bed, if she didn't cover the stippled concrete walls the freeze became unbearable, even with the stove's heat.

Oatmeal done, Ember carried a bowl to her mom along with a mug of fresh water. She grabbed her own food and climbed in next to Susan, focused on the animated antics to mask anxiety and keep from checking how far into dawn the day had moved.

"Are you home today?" Susan's eyes drooped and Ember eased her dishes away.

"I have things to do." Susan didn't react to Ember's canned response.

By the time she cleaned up breakfast, enough sunlight brightened the room that Ember flicked off the electric lights. Her mom had sunk deeper into her pillows and cartoons had shifted to the local news - the only news.

She was ready to leave. Ember had kept calm for her mom's sake, but with nothing left to do, she'd soon pace a hole in the floor. Better to face things in the sunlight and gain an advantage in the meantime. After that, find a more secure place to hide than her dead end house.

Susan's skeletal hand shot out and wrapped around Ember's narrow wrist. Ember focused on her mom's stormy grey eyes, judged the expanse between Susan's lids and thinned lips to see anxiety buzzed within her, but would not be debilitating.

"Stay away from the magic," Susan begged.

"I know," Ember assured her mom.

"He tricked me. Hurt me. Stay away from magic."

Ember flinched at the mention of her father, a Wizard who'd broken the law, and then somehow left Trifecta right as Ember was being born. She'd wondered in the past if he'd had the same skill she had with the barrier, but he hadn't returned, and she couldn't get out. It wasn't a question worth losing sleep over. He was gone.

Ember placed a gentle kiss on her mom's forehead and

smoothed thin brown hair back toward her messy bun until Susan let her go.

"Get some rest," Ember said.

Part of their building did not add to their living space, but held a separate entrance to the tunnels. She had used it to return home last night, but this morning her path kept her top side. She hopped along the hill and landed in the street. Hands in her pockets, she scanned the area. To the right lay a gated, disintegrated road into the forest. It also led to the Fae.

Ember turned left toward the well-maintained, idyllic suburb of human homes. The neighborhood was planned so each house faced the valley, maple and birch trees blocking the neighbors and downtown from that picturesque view. A few of the local pines had squeezed back onto some of their land with help of the wildlife and peeked in green towers above the fiery shades of autumn. She pulled up her hood, curled her shoulders and kept her eyes lowered as she made her way up the street.

A door squeaked in imitation of the happy birds singing from the interspersed forest. Ember angled her vision in that direction, sure it was nothing, cautious nevertheless.

This time it was something. Damn it. Aaron Harwell loped over the white-painted stairs of his porch, across the red-brick path to his gate where he vaulted the pickets.

The reason for his athleticism? His eyes never left her, as if he'd known she'd be along and had waited. Had he discerned what she had done to the cars last night?

"Where's Nicu?"

Not what she expected, and something she didn't care to know given the current circumstances.

"Hello to you, too. How did you sleep?" She used a sickly sweet tone she hoped hid the hitch in her voice and, if lucky, would deter him.

"I need to talk to him. He always pops up around you."

"Yep. True stalker material. Do you think I should report

him to the police?" Aaron's brow furrowed. Apparently he didn't like jokes.

"This is serious, Ember."

Ember shook off the odd sensation that tickled across her nape with the use of her name. Few people used her name. No humans did, other than her mom. It was... peculiar and unsettling to have someone talk to her as a person, not just the Trimarked.

"Walk toward Fae lands. I'm sure he, or another Fae, will show up." Aaron flinched and shoved his fists into jean pockets. Hunched shoulders showed he wasn't ready to go that far.

"Brandt disappeared."

Oh. Fade.

Ember swallowed hard, shook her hair forward to hide the sudden pallor of her cheeks. This would go down as her worst mistake, ever.

"Maybe he fell off." She tried not to choke on the words meaning off the end of the world, out of Trifecta, and bonus points for being truthful.

"This is not funny," Aaron spoke through gritted teeth. "He got into a fight with your Fae boyfriend before he disappeared."

Well, shit, at least Nicu wasn't aware of what happened and helping Aaron might get the human off her back. Then again, if Edan had told his leader what he'd learned, then drawing Fae attention to herself for the sake of getting Aaron to leave her alone would not be the best plan. Ignoring the situation proved pointless when Aaron slipped to the front of Ember to stop her.

"Do you understand? Brandt is missing. I want to find him. I think Nicu can help. Now, where is he?"

He spoke as if to a three-year-old, or somebody stupid, but anger eluded her. Instead, she fought off an image of Brandt, and tried not to remember the shock and horror on his face when he realized what she'd done. What Edan now knew she was capable of. That which Aaron Harwell could not find out.

Her fingertips patted her thighs, directed her nerves so she kept her words steady.

"I'm not the one who stalks, if you recall."

"Fine." Aaron danced a few feet back, freed his hands for balance. "Nicu!" He shouted across the neighborhood, into this world of family homes guarded by gilded trees and picketed gates. "Nicu!" As if Fae answered human summons.

Ember held her breath, nerves and disbelief focused on the boy in the middle of the street making a fool of himself. Tension coiled in her stomach, then punched between clenched lips in the form of an incredulous bark of laughter. Aaron stopped mid-inhale, his open mouth slammed into a scowl.

"He's my friend."

Not so funny. Ember lowered her chin over the tight bruise at her neck.

"In that case." She stepped around Aaron and kept walking.

Aaron caught up. Ember huffed but didn't increase her speed. It wasn't like she could outrun him.

"Okay, I get it. He was a jerk last night. He was drunk. I swear, he's a good guy."

"Yep. The poster child for a great education and closet rapist. But as long as it's only the Trimarked girl…."

To his credit, Aaron blanched.

They reached a T-shaped intersection. The perpendicular street to the right remained unbroken with a solid stretch of pavement, and to the left lay a pockmarked, vehicle death trap. Aaron's feet swung to cross the smooth black pathway that marked his domain. Ember watched him go a few strides, then picked her way across the seldom used path toward the Circle.

"Hey, what?" Aaron called behind her. A groan escaped her when the sound of his footsteps turned back in her direction.

"Where are you going? Those are Witch lands." He almost grabbed her arm in his distress. Cute.

Ember flashed silver eyes, a challenge in her feral smile. "Well, Aaron, if you want to find your friend, you must learn how to take risks."

Aaron contemplated the path before them. A line of boarded-up, weathered houses marked the end of the human neighborhood. Bushes once pruned into decorative living hedges now over grew their beds and hid the old sidewalk until even these last signs of pre-convergence gave way to the forest.

"Do you think they'll know something about Brandt?"

Well, fading fades. She'd messed up that one. Aaron crunched to her side, hands tucked into his letter jacket, then back to his jean pockets, then out again to cross and hold beneath opposite arms.

"I've never been there. Be my guide?" he asked.

"Verge, no. You're on your own."

"Okay. I'll follow."

Ember considered punching him in the gut, but figured he'd still scramble after her, if a few more feet behind. Not worth the energy. She continued toward the Witch's compound and stomped a little louder to hide the echo of a second set of footsteps, an attempt to pretend, at least, that she wasn't being forced to endure his company.

8

EMBER

*T*he Pine River cut the Circle's territory in half. The barrier butted up against stark cliffs denoting the sharp rise of the mountain. Though this resulted in the fewest livable acres, it had not deterred the Witches in their choice of the industrial zone, built on the most level ground in all Trifecta. It needed them the most, they said, and no one else had been eager to take it once they realized life couldn't go on as normal.

The coven had demolished the old roads. Concrete chunks were piled along with other raw materials waiting for transfer to an empty warehouse. They had turned every hard won, cleared patch into something wonderful. Car parks became flower beds divided by paths and pillars of stacked, potted herbs. Factories converted into vine-covered apartment homes with blooms brightening up the surfaces. Carved stone walkways wound through the gardens without a straight line in sight.

Aaron gawked as he stepped from broken road to a manicured, gravel separation between entropy and design. His eyes danced in response to the beauty and chaos of the ever changing neighborhood. Ember waited for his attention to leave the organized reconstruction and listened for the audible choke the moment he saw the mages themselves.

This race did not believe in subtlety. Everyone had a shade of red hair. The color held special meaning for the Witches. Red represented passion, blood, life, love, and creation's beginnings. Few sported natural ginger tresses. Burgundy appeared to be the trend, though Ember caught a few magentas and fiery orange hues. Their clothes ranged from flow wraps to leather pants and tied cotton shirts, fitted tops and flowing skirts or wide legged slacks. Whatever they wore was organic, colorful, and created a garden of people alongside their berries and roses.

They were unashamed of their power. Even with strangers among them, gentle fingers coaxed magic to speed the growth of sprouts. Stones rippled along a laid path. The Wizard manipulating them frowned and gestured to encourage unique patterns as he debated which to choose. A group of three mages Worked over a carved fountain and encouraged water from deep within the earth to spring up for a natural, magical source.

Aaron couldn't decide where to look, and the way he blanched or glanced at his feet suggested he wasn't sure he should.

"Haven't you seen a Witch before?" Ember mocked. Aaron shook his head.

Ember's amusement smashed into irritation. Of course not. Witches visited town to find people who needed the items they uncovered and wanted to repurpose. Witches were the source for machine parts, responsible for revitalized soil that gave human gardens added longevity, grew and sold much of the produce and wove at least half of the new cloth found in Trifecta. But no, golden boy had never seen a Witch.

Finished with him, Ember lengthened her stride and headed beyond the reclaimed land toward the not yet touched mess at the back. She had her own mystery to figure out.

"Hey, wait! How do I find out about Brandt?"

"I suggest asking questions."

"But... but who?"

Ember turned, elbows at her hips, palms flipped out between them to show she had nothing for him. "As I'm not in the habit of looking for lost people, I can't help you. Start over there." She gestured in a random direction, then left Aaron to his own devices.

The colors of cultivation gave way to heavy grays deeper into the Circle. Perfumed air soured with the off gassing of old, burnt fossil fuels, mold and filth. Cats lounged in whatever sun there was between broken buildings and mounds of clutter, soaking up energy for the coming night when they earned their keep by catching rodents, cockroaches and other pests.

Rounded, organized heaps of small metals, wires, concrete, cut stone and more gave way to precarious mountains of unsorted materials. Here, Ember checked every opening, tilted her head to listen for and identify the softest sounds. Devi moved often depending on her task and where she found the most solitude around the reclamation efforts of others.

Today, Ember's eyes located Devi before her ears. In a large garage, barrels of reclaimed waste oil stacked against the wall, a few of them open. A line of mismatched tables held a chemistry set, bowls of powders, jars of cut herbs, layered texts labeled with scientific titles, even a few ancient tomes that had Faded in alongside the Witches.

Devi sat wrapped in a large, deep blue wool poncho lined with bright green and white. Tied high on her waist with a hemp belt, the folded sleeves left her arms free, stacks of gem-laded bracelets twined around her forearms. Three books lay open before her, a Witch tome, one chemistry from this realm and a notebook, a familiar pose that meant she sought to cross reference the science of nature and the science of magic, her frown heavy with the struggle.

"Still trying to clean used oil?" Ember asked.

"Yes," she answered. "The Ternate Star has risen and I'm hoping its rumored ability to affect change might help."

"Ternate?"

"Hmm." Devi continued her work. "Three stars that form a group impossible to chart as it only pops over the horizon during autumn, but not on any kind of schedule. Funny story, the Fae call it the Chaos Star, so it is my favorite."

"A fairy tale comes to mind, making changes with powers of three. It doesn't end well for the maiden."

"Luckily, I'm not one to make bargains that don't finish in my favor."

Ember cleared her throat. The segue had her tapping staccato in debate. Move right in or wait a minute?

"Just ask," Devi inferred. "And stop drumming before you get arthritis."

Ember linked her hands together and squeezed for courage. The problems always came after the asking.

"I need to learn how to deal with a Fae."

"You handle them pretty well on your own." Devi stopped pursuing lines of text. Mint-green irises as sharp and bright as gems rose as her pencil fell. "You mean negotiate."

Ember kept her fingers still by forcing them into tight hip pockets. Devi's steady contemplation became a pressure against skin as the Witch looked over Ember's stiffened form.

"You can't pay for that. You don't have time. True understanding takes years."

"I have something that's enough for a crash course."

Devi pushed out from the table and crossed her arms. Ember meant to allow Devi to look at her tattoo in exchange for instruction on how to talk to Edan. The Witch had been asking Ember for years if she could study the mark, not with any promise to free Ember from it, but because Devi wanted to learn. She was a scholar at heart, one that studied all kinds of magic and used her knowledge to go after difficult tasks, such as turning spent motor oil into something usable. A chance to examine Fae Ink was a hefty item for trade in Devi's mind. It didn't take long for the Witch's eyes to light up with understanding. Just as quickly, Ember watched her interest tighten into suspicion.

"What have you done, Ember Lee? Why are you desperate to bargain with a Fae? And it had better not be Nicu. I refuse to help you with him, even at the price you offer. I will not give that Fae more of you than he already has."

"Not Nicu. Edan. He needs my cooperation with something and I don't want to go into it blind."

A softened truth. Devi would know she wasn't getting the entire story. Ember wanted an outline version of how to bargain with the most manipulative race in the realms. Her trade was fair, so for Devi, learning why Ember needed the lesson would mean she'd owe Ember something else.

Devi stood and swung the chair out in front of her, suggesting the 'why' would not be cost efficient for the Witch.

"Sit," Devi said.

"Information first."

"I can multitask."

Ember's footsteps scuffed over the dirty floor. Ember swallowed hard, spun on her heel and looked at the small, open door. For a moment, she debated using it, then sat. What was the harm in showing Devi her tattoo for the ability to stay in a safe place, and get help with Edan?

Ember forced herself to stop fidgeting when Devi flicked her shoulder.

"Hoodies off," Devi ordered. Ember gripped the hems of the hoodies and slipped them over her head to keep them bunched against her chest. The cloth of the waffle henley wasn't thick enough to block out the chill, so the layered hoodies would stay on in front.

Devi released her own messy top bun with sharp, firm movements, then used the tie to wrap up Ember's mane into a compact knot. The breeze touched her nape, and she swallowed twists of anxiety that tightened her core. She kept her hair long to block the Trimark from view. Yet, this had been the deal. For now, she couldn't hide behind the millions of dark strands.

"Who choked you?"

Ember's fists clenched, her thoughts torn from the back of her neck to the front. She couldn't see the bruise but felt the stiff fibers whenever she moved. "A human kid. I took care of it."

Devi hummed, her attention returned to the business of studying Binding Ink. "Have you ever looked at this?"

"I haven't grown eyes that can swing around, no," Ember answered dryly.

"There are mirrors."

Ember stayed silent. The only mirror she had hung in her small bathroom, spider-webbed and foggy with age, useless for checking out the bruise on the front of her neck, much less the tattoo on the back.

Devi's fingers caressed the lines as she described something Ember had never glimpsed, but knew by heart.

"Half a butterfly's wing, or a closed wing from the side, I suppose. The pentacle overlaps, the frame integrated with the delicate design of the wing." The gentle rasp of Devi's nail scratched out a star surrounded by a circle, with a deeper scrape through it. "The circle is pulled through, slashing across to break the lines of the pentacle. Control." Devi spat the last word as if it were a curse.

"I didn't expect it to be so intricate. It's beautiful." The reluctant words pressed through her lips in a murmur. "And not entirely Fae. A Witch helped with the pentacle and hanging embellishments. Hmm."

Devi peered into jars and bowls along the table, gathered a pinch of this and a carafe of that, and moved into her part of the trade.

"The first rule of making a bargain with a Fae. Don't."

Ember huffed and shifted toward the young woman behind her, eyes narrowed in accusation.

"Don't be stupid." Devi set down the ingredients she collected. On a shallow plate, she lit a few incenses and masked the dank odors of the warehouse and its contents. In an empty bowl, she poured water, cedar chips, sage, something that might have been rosemary, a leaf that smelled of mint, plus another few crumpled and sprinkled selections Ember couldn't name. "Of course, that is the first rule. Fae are incredibly gifted with speech and have an intricate handle on languages a human could never hope to grasp."

"Good thing I'm not human," Ember drawled.

"Part human."

As the mixture settled, Devi stroked the small charms along her arms. As if by touch alone, the Witch slipped a stone from its hemp cage, then another. Ember kept a sharp eye over Devi's deft movements, not sure what she might see but not wanting to blindly participate, either. Quartz, amethyst, and something streaked in gold with dark brown deposits spotting the surface. Devi held the stones stable between the fingers on her left hand while she returned to the herb blend on the table.

"If you can get out of making a bargain, that is your best choice. However, if Edan is intent on getting whatever help he needs from you, listen closely. Do not, under any circumstances, accept anything. To accept something is to increase the price you have to pay. Do not assume an offer is tit for tat. It is not."

Devi moved the mortar into a beam of sunlight and reached for her pestle. As she ground the herbs, she held the three stones over the bowl to filter the light.

"Be very, very careful what you demand. Demanding is not accepting. It is not asking. Demanding puts your offer against his. Which leads to always speaking in absolutes. There should be no agreement with the Fae, simply an end to demands."

Without fire, the mixture smoked. Ember shifted in her

chair, away from the table. She flinched when a blue flame burst into the mortar.

"Stop being a baby. It's only witchflame. All light and no bite."

Ember centered herself in the chair and closed her eyes after deciding she didn't need to see everything Devi was doing.

When something smooth touched her neck, the chill surprised her. Devi smeared a paste over the Trimark, the soft chant of her words a warm balm that followed.

An arc of power zapped over Ember, the brand burned through the ice of Devi's concoction. Electricity pinched against her skin and jarred through the nerves in her spine. Glass shattered across the table with the sound of Ember's throat-ripping screech.

Water doused over her nape from the silver carafe Devi held in her hand.

Gasping, Ember collapsed onto her own lap, arms limp at her sides.

"Ember Lee," Devi rasped. "This mark is not only on your skin. The Fae connected it to something, constrained you again somewhere else. You must be very, very careful."

Ember supported herself with forearms pressed against her thighs as she sat hunched over, not sure what she should do with that information. Nothing had changed, not even knowing the Fae had bound her. What did an extra layer matter when the result remained the same?

Devi draped a cloth over Ember's neck, then spoke a spell for heat and warmth that drew the water from her clothing.

"Is it bad?" Ember asked.

"It is bad, but not in the way you ask. Your skin is fine, perfect. There is no sign of contact. The reaction came from the binding around whatever they attached to your mark." Devi's finger pad stroked the back of Ember's neck, gentle and cooling while her opposite hand pulled the hair ribbon free.

Ember's tresses descended to cover the tattoo once again, her shoulders softened in relief.

"Thank you for your payment," Devi said. The pause that followed stretched so long Ember regained most of her strength. She put the dried hoodies back in place, pulled her hair free, and turned in her chair to see Devi staring out the open door.

Devi's thick sigh indicated any conclusions she drew were not as satisfying as she wished. "I have more to learn and as I do, we may find I am in your debt."

Ember swallowed the bitter lump in her throat, forced herself to stand, though her knees shook. She faced the Witch.

"Let's hope I never have to cash in." Devi nodded, eyes still unfocused. After a moment, Ember dropped the damp cloth on the chair, turned and walked weak-legged from Devi's workroom. No need to make things awkward.

9

AARON

*W*ell. Fade, that hadn't gone as planned. Aaron did not understand what turned Ember's irritation into anger, yet there she went.

Left on his own, he returned to observing the most incredible space he'd ever seen. In school they'd learned about the industrial park, pre-Witches, through books and photographs. The factories provided a reminder of humanity's strength and cleverness, their ability to use technology to conquer a natural world in a way magic never could.

But, wow, the Witches were creating miracles - or magic - with the leftovers of the old era of industry. The thought of magic shot a shudder through his chest and Aaron rocked back on his heels, aware of the sideways stares from the mages.

Why had he followed Ember here, again?

Brandt. Verge. That idiot had to stop drinking. Trouble with his long-time friend, sure, Aaron was used to that. Graffiti, joy rides, skipping school, sneaking a blunt after practice — always after because funked up lungs killed their performance. And the End of the World joust. All part of growing up in a bubble.

Getting onto a Fae's radar was new. Aaron waltzing into gnome land to find his friend, definitely outside the usual.

Whoops, Witch, not gnome. He glanced around and wondered if mind reading was a thing here, and if human slang that compared the mages to pointy-hatted yard decorations irritated them.

No evil glares, no fingers waved in his direction, more backs faced him than not. Okay. He was probably okay.

Honestly, though, since he was here, he should ask someone something.

Aaron meandered to an older man with knees deep into a garden while he moved soil around to make room for the potted plants at his side. He didn't look up when Aaron's shadow covered his work.

"Hi, um. I'm looking for a friend."

The Wizard looked up and shaded his eyes.

"And you think this person is here? We are not actually in the habit of kidnapping humans for sacrifices."

"What? No, no, that's not what I meant. I mean, he's gone but I don't know where to look and I thought —"

"Scrying," the Wizard huffed. His sneer melted into distaste. "Leona might help if you have something to trade."

"Oh." Aaron scowled at the ground, not having brought money. The man's lips twisted into a take-him-as-a-sucker smile.

"Cash is not the only currency."

Aaron didn't know what that meant, but shrugged and figured he could talk to this Leona to find out.

"Okay. Where is she?"

"Go to the greenhouse." He gestured as Ember had, but this time Aaron assumed the Wizard had given him a helpful direction. Maybe.

Aaron picked his way around the village, careful not to run into anyone, over anything, and to stay clear of anyone who looked like they were working. Not knowing much about

Witches, he wasn't sure what offenses might get him cursed, or worse, kicked out without answers.

Not clear on the exact location of the greenhouse, Aaron strained his eyes to find it. He doubted the humans of the past built a glass building for plants amongst, well, plants that made things.

Beyond the first set of vast buildings, Aaron caught a flash of over-bright sunshine up the cross street. A glass enclosed structure protruded from the building on the left and had caused the reflection. Though age fogged the lower windows, the upper panes shone clear where they climbed four stories high and curved back toward the brick at the top.

The double door sprouted long U-shaped handles. He peeked in first and knocked, then went inside.

"Shut the door behind you." The voice held the melody of water and the depth of forest. A shiver tickled Aaron's spine as he followed instructions that left him firmly inside. He wasn't worried, per se. He was a human male and protected by the Laws of Convergence. Yet, he was still a human on Witch land and that didn't happen often.

"Over here."

Aaron peered around the multi-layered garden. Rich, thick earth and flowering blooms filtered through his nose. The claustrophobic entrance narrowed further into cramped walkways between shelves and tables piled high with plants or trees in pots. The cacophony created nowhere to look with a million things to see. He stepped deeper to find the person who spoke.

"Yeah, I'm looking for Leona."

The woman chuckled and, though Aaron's shoulders bunched, he realized there was no vehemence in it but genuine amusement. He rolled his neck and shook out his fingers like he did before a game and tried to relax.

"Come on." A garden-gloved hand peeked out from beside a large potted fern.

Aaron hop-stepped to catch up before he lost her again.

When he approached the junction, he found a woman his height, her carrot orange hair twisted up and twined through the center of a tan, woven hat as if she planned to be out in the sun. She wore bright green flared leggings and a ruffled blouse speckled with so many intense, floral tones it looked like a painting gone wrong.

"I hear the Trimarked Child brought you."

"Yes, well." He wondered what counted as a lie and if it mattered to her. "I kinda followed her when she told me where she was going. I'm looking for a friend."

"A noble cause." Aaron gasped when her sharp, amethyst eyes came into view, catching the light in their depths as if composed of the polished gem. "A genuine friend is hard to find."

"Y-yes." A slight bounce began at his toes. "His name is Brandt and—"

"I cannot tell you of things beyond the Veil," she dismissed with a hand wave.

"Oh. I thought you meant—"

"I promise you, I'm not the one mistaking the problem." Aaron frowned at the intimation he mistook the question when he had asked it.

"Let's see." Those purple eyes left him and scanned the field of potted plants. "What can help? Not fickleness," she spoke, caressing a bunch of yellow puff balls on long stems. "Not pride. We'll keep looking."

"Okay, but what are we doing? The man in the garden mentioned scrying."

The Witch smiled. "Well, we could, but like I said, beyond the Veil. So, we will work on something else. Aha, here we go. Arborvitae." The bush reached to the four story high ceiling. She trimmed a branch and kept moving.

"Some fern," she agreed, as if in a debate with someone. "But for color…" Leona turned to face him, shoulders squared with his, and looked him over top to bottom, bottom to top.

Aaron squirmed, not knowing what she saw, though he felt confident it wasn't his letterman's jacket.

"Huh." Leona blinked, and then squinted into a slight lean. "Oh. I see what we need." She grabbed a basket from under a table and returned to her task with new vigor.

She picked three different tree blossoms, then a few herbs he recognized because of the abrupt change of smell from fragrant to sharp. Next, she gathered a few long-stemmed flowers in full bloom. She stopped in front of the roses, touched between the pink and the white. "That may be too much to ask." She turned to him with her harvest.

"Ah, I'm not looking for a bouquet," he said.

The woman's earthy, musical laugh felt too intimate with the walls of plants around them.

"Of course not." She gestured once again for him to follow. With a huff of confusion, Aaron did as he was told, pretty sure he would not get what he wanted, while completely certain he didn't want to offend a Witch.

Leona led him to a counter height wooden table covered with a round of linen cloth, knives, scissors, a variety of bowls and odd, thick sticks. She laid out her bounty over an empty stretch, fingered the creamy gem hanging from her earring, then pulled the loop out of her ear with a quick tug. With efficient motions, she placed a white marble bowl onto a spot in the sun, and set a glass pitcher of clean water beside it.

With a quiet song on her lips, Leona held the stone in the light, splashed a small amount of water over and around it into the bowl, then returned her earring. She didn't use the whole of anything she picked, but combed over, pet and popped off pieces.

"All of Nature holds magic. Witches and Wizards sense it as a force through all Created things, blood without a pulse that can be removed either with deep magic Work, or by crushing. With crushing, you have the added benefit of being able to blend the nuances of each piece of Nature, which is why we chose so many components for your friendship request."

"Like the water being pulled for the fountain was magic."

"Ah, you saw that? I'm glad to hear they've gotten that far. And no, the water itself isn't magic. There is magic in the water that the Witches and Wizards are manipulating, and then the water simply follows."

The fragments mounded in the bowl and soaked up water. Leona slipped the black gem from her opposite ear and doused it with another pour of from the pitcher. She mashed everything up into a goopy brown paste.

"Take off your shirt."

"Wait-what?"

The Witch turned to him as she grabbed her bowl.

"You're looking for a friend."

"Yes," he agreed, the word drawn out over the nervous presumption she didn't mean Brandt.

"Raise your shirt."

Aaron's fingers shook as he unzipped his jacket and shrugged it off, careful to lay it on a clean section of the counter. He tugged his charcoal colored tee from the one place he tucked it at the front of his belt, then pulled it off. The Witch grinned.

"A healthy boy, I see."

Aaron flushed and turned his head with a small cough. Leona snickered, dipped her hands in the goo, and reached out to paint Aaron's chest. He tilted his chin against his neck to watch her draw out a triangle with dots at the vertices and swirls inside and out.

"Now, Fae need not speak while they Work, but therein lies the beauty of differences. I'm going to start a chant, one that will help direct the magic of plants into your inherent magic."

"I don't have magic."

Leona tsked. "You weren't listening. All of Nature has

magic. Not all beings can access it. Unfortunately, dear, humans do not sense or use magic. I explained the plants, so you have an idea of what is happening. At this point, I will sing words you know, but will not recognize as they interlace with magic, but it's nothing to be afraid of."

With that, Leona's eyes drifted closed and her lips murmured over a song as soft and warm as springtime sunshine. Whatever words she spoke became another musical note as they drifted through his ears. The Witch pulled an orange stone from one of her bracelets as if she knew each one of them intimately. Holding the gem between her thumb and palm, Leona raised her hand parallel with her artwork, closed her eyes, and sang.

The plant goo flashed. Aaron braced himself against the pressure of a shove, though she hadn't made a move. The light dimmed, and the design sank into his pores, disappeared from view.

Leona sighed and shook her head with a smile.

"Well, candles might have supported the Work, but better to keep flames far from my babies."

"Um. So. Magic?" Aaron stumbled. Leona winked and cleaned up unused plant pieces.

"It's what Witches do."

"But the Laws—"

Leona pinned him with a sharp gaze. "Did you come to me for help?"

"Y-yes."

"Did you walk with me and tell me of your needs?"

"Yes."

"Did you participate willingly?" Aaron stopped himself from saying no because, in truth, he had followed every instruction.

"Yes. Just uncomfortable."

"Well." She tapped his cheek. "You are a first timer. You should put your clothes back on and find your friend."

"So you know where he is?" Aaron grabbed his shirt and threw it on, flush with hope her spell had given her a lead on Brandt.

"He? No he, but I imagine she finished her own task and I'm sure you won't want to miss her." Aaron stared at Leona, features slack as he ruffled his curls.

"The Trimarked Child."

"Oh!" Aaron caught his jacket and rushed for the door, skidded back from a crossing when he'd passed the main path out.

Not that Ember was his friend by a long shot, but she was still his only link to finding Brandt as his journey down the gnome-hole had proved fruitless. He did not want to lose her.

*U*ncertain if her visit with Devi had turned out successful, Ember passed through the human ruins and the completed part of the Circle, focused inward, the corner of her bottom lip held between her teeth.

Don't negotiate with the Fae. Rule one. The only way to do that was to throw herself out.

The thing was, it wasn't possible. Ember discovered five years ago she could tap out a particular pattern onto the barrier, a rat-a-tat, a knock on a door. She'd been tossing a ball above her head in a gradual arc toward the invisible wall she leaned against. The trees offered shade on that hot day, and the wind hit her back through the barrier, free to move through the very thing that held her upright. The toy returned on the same bend, man-made things as unable to pass as their makers, and she caught it. She'd been proud of that trick. Though, as her only entertainment, perfection was all but guaranteed.

One hand tossed, one hand stretched out against the barrier for no particular reason.

Tap-tap-tap, tap-tap-tap. Pointer, middle, ring finger, then reversed.

Her ball hadn't returned. Ember twisted around, then

caught the dark blue of the rubber from the corner of her eye. Gaped. The ball had rolled to rest in a refuge of pine needles, and a slice of sunlight spotlit where it rested on the outside.

From there, Ember tried to tap herself out, press herself out. She pounded with her fist, knocked with her feet, but only her fingers ever created a unique opening. Ember started testing how long the portal remained open. She collected trash on her walks to see how many things she could toss through, how far away she could run, turn and throw something out, all before it closed again.

That's how Chase had discovered her secret. Ember thought she'd been safe in that quiet space of forest, had always double checked she wasn't being followed by Witch or Fae before she experimented. She must have gotten careless because Chase slipped past her guard and found her throwing chicken bones. She'd been too afraid to leave, frozen with uncertainty.

"Can people go through?" he asked.

She shrugged. "I can't."

"Maybe you're just supposed to hold it open."

So started their odd relationship, with her passing a few of his crew through to get outside intel. Ember negotiated for food, clothes, blankets, things she and her mom needed. Ember had been so relieved Chase kept her secret, she never cared why he wanted his particular favors.

Never imagined she'd be grateful for it, either, and she shuddered at the memory of his promise to have his guys on the outside control Brandt.

"Hey."

Ember jumped, turned with hands halfway raised into fists. Aaron backed up and surprise rounded his features.

Ah, the other side of the problem. Ember resumed her walk, eyes forward as they crossed the gravel leading to the human neighborhood.

"Nothing about Brandt, thanks for asking."

"I didn't," she snapped back. Aaron croaked half of a word, thought better of it, and settled his lips into a frown.

"Didn't get what you wanted, either, huh?"

Ember scowled. His words hit home.

"I don't know what else I expected," she said. A spell. Concrete advice. Not a list of rules so ridiculous they must be accurate. What did it even mean, state what you want until you both stop talking? How did you know what the agreement was by the time you finished? How was that nonsense worth a look at her magic-made tattoo? Ember kicked a rock that only rolled a few inches into a depression in the broken road. About as far as she'd gotten, too.

"Does Nicu check in with you?"

A headache blossomed over Ember's brow. Not this again.

"He doesn't. I don't even see him most of the time. They're not really my babysitters."

"Oh. I heard… I guess we all thought he was always with you. I mean, in the stories he's invisible until you're messed with, then he's very much there and one pissed pixie."

"If only. You are messing me and he is nowhere to be found." *Thankfully*, but not that word out loud.

"Well, yeah, but I won't hurt you. I just want to find Brandt."

Ember watched Aaron for a moment from the corner of her eye and tried to figure out if he was for real or not.

"Are all humans like you?"

Aaron whipped his head around, his brow twisted in confusion.

"What do you—" His mouth shut and his eyes widened as he puzzled it out. "Oh."

Yeah, oh. When you're deemed invisible, when no race claimed you, you didn't hang out with that many people. At least she hadn't had to say it.

Ember sighed herself out of reverie, and looked around to see how close they were to his house, how soon she might get rid of him. They'd passed the white and blue structure and were closer to her home than his. She wanted to demand why he still walked with her, turned to confront him, then froze.

Edan stood in the shadows of the forest, leaned against one of the outer trees, eyes focused on the road. Not inconspicuous, meaning he'd planned for her to see that he waited.

Ember swallowed despite a dry mouth. Well. She wasn't ready for him. Ember gripped Aaron's elbow and pulled him up the hill, not to her house, but to the side door that opened to a part of the building separate from her home. Edan wouldn't approach her if she had Aaron with her, so the human had to stay. Beyond that, there was one place the Fae would not follow.

"What are you doing?"

"I have an idea." Her words chased each other. It was more of a reaction than a plan, but she went with it, anyway. Ember pulled the monochrome door open.

"About Brandt?"

Fading Brandt!

"I thought of someone who can help."

Never mind that she meant someone to help her, not him.

What Chase would do about Aaron was yet to be seen. Topsiders were not welcome where they headed. She led them into the staircase, ready to find out.

11

EMBER

*C*eiling-mounted solar powered lights cast a soft glow that fell short of filling the tunnel. It took a moment to adjust to the gloom. Ember was familiar with the passage and could walk while her eyes dilated, but she paused for Aaron's sake.

When the rectangular lines of the concrete passageway came into focus, she moved. Aaron hovered, never too far, as if an invisible tether kept them close. Even more than at the Circle, he appeared uncomfortable, which was fine with Ember. Perhaps he wouldn't notice her own freak out over Edan, not that he had any clue how she behaved.

They plodded over damp concrete. Aaron's steps pound out a harsh cadence. Ember's softer step whispered more often with her shorter stride. She didn't mind the pace. As certain as she felt Edan wouldn't follow, she did not want to encourage her current unlucky streak.

The pair reached another metal door and Ember pounded the side of her fist against it. The buzz of many voices filled the tunnel when the door eased open to the clubhouse. Formerly a large holding tank, the space had been meant to capture too much snowmelt or flood waters. The once yearly events had disappeared over time, long before the Fade. Now it served as an exclusive hideaway, and the current gatekeeper's amused brown eyes narrowed when he spotted Aaron.

"Why did you bring a bouncer to the party?" Keegan demanded.

"He wants to learn to box."

"Cross training." Aaron played along.

"Right. Because pretty boy soccer players are great at getting punch drunk." Keegan mimicked a jab to his own cheek. "But sure. Why not? Ember never brings guests."

Keegan threw open the door and invited them into the large, circular room with a flourish. Ember took her first deep breath since Edan and wondered how long she could hide here. Aaron was drop-jaw awed once again by a place he'd never suspected existed within Trifecta.

They had separated the generous space into a boxing gym to the left and a pub to the right, complete with a kitchen. Couches and heavy armchairs danced in the center of the room, pulled to wherever the current occupant required. Well-used round tables and mismatched chairs spread out in front of the kitchen and a few dark wood, patched vinyl booths pressed against the outer wall in between doors.

There were ten entrances and exits into the Clubhouse. Each led to a different tunnel of the concrete labyrinth that continued to multiple spots within the lower half of Trifecta. Ember had used this system last night to get home. Passage through any door was limited to help keep the movements of their society secret, and to keep topsiders from interfering with the few places the Halfers called theirs.

Halfers weren't the only ones who found refuge underground. People whose lifestyle or gender didn't match up to their topsider parents' expectations made their way here. Runaways from homes where fists were the preferred method of communication were brought in, as well.

The community was almost as big as any of the three that

lived topside. Despite the terminology, the outcasts didn't live underground. They squatted in between the established races in the old maintenance spaces and abandoned houses, using the tunnels to travel, or in the Clubhouse's case, hangout en masse.

After a quick scan, Ember found Chase in a semi-circular booth. He displayed shaggy red-gold hair that hinted at Witch genes along with his dark green eyes. He never told her about his parents, and she never asked, respecting the rules of the game.

When Chase noticed her, a brow raised in question and summons. Ember checked on Aaron. Keegan tugged him toward the ring. Not interested in getting between the boxer and his newest student, Ember passed by the makeshift kitchen, wove around and between the crowd until she pulled out a chair.

"I can't watch the room if you sit there," Chase stopped her. Ember took a spot next to him on the curved bench instead. "Are you here to train?"

"The ring looks taken, and I didn't bring my gym bag."

"Self defense is priceless. Besides, you're good for it." His confidence in her ability to pay shot a shiver of surprise into her chest. "If I were you, I'd be more worried about the cost of bringing a topsider here than me getting a laugh in while you try to take Keegan."

The weight of his words swept away the astonishment, and she wondered if he would use that to talk numbers. How much did she owe him for Brandt? For dragging Aaron to the Clubhouse?

Chase cultivated silence into an uncomfortable atmosphere while he watched Keegan give Aaron a crash course. Before long, they stripped off their shirts and put on pads for a sink-or-swim match, no training wheels for the interloper.

"He's handsome, at least, despite the charm on his chest."

"You can see a spell?" Ember straightened to glimpse Aaron's uncovered skin but couldn't find evidence of a mark.

Chase spun his glass and lowered his volume to float beneath the noise.

"I've been honing my skills."

"Can you tell what it is?" she asked.

"Not precisely, though it has a be kind to others vibe. Did you know he visited a Witch?"

"Yeah." Ember licked her lips. "We just came from there."

"Together?"

"Sort of. We talked to different mages. He's been tailing me today."

"Is he giving you shit about the cars?"

"Brandt," Ember answered. Chase's face fell into neutral lines. "He assumes sticking with me will help him find Nicu. He thinks Nicu knows about Brandt."

"You want me to send him away?"

"No. I can handle him by myself. I just needed... time."

"Hmm." Chase returned to the entertainment in the boxing ring.

Ember chuckled when Aaron took his first hit with the grace of a puppy. The golden boy shook it off to her surprise, raised his gloves and doubled down.

"He's a quick learner," Chase murmured. He sipped his drink, then offered it to her. Ember hesitated, but accepted the full glass. After a mouthful of water, she tried to hand it back.

"Keep it," he insisted. "Germs." Ember blinked at him, drank again and placed the cup on the table, nervous about the gift.

Her fingers drew in the condensation outside the green plastic. She didn't know what to do if she couldn't escape here without worrying over hidden costs.

Aaron called time after five minutes of lessons spaced out by bouts of punches. The opponents tapped gloves, and the match ended. Keegan led Aaron to the kitchen for a drink, then over to Chase. The boys were wet with sweat. The way

Keegan shoulder bumped Aaron, a new bromance had been born.

"Can I keep him?" Keegan asked.

"Bouncers don't make good pets," Chase admonished. "Can't house train them and all."

Aaron's easy going manner stiffened, though Keegan snorted a laugh.

"No joke, boss, but no problem. Can Ember bring him by again?"

Chase shrugged. "That's her deal. Now leave him with his owner and give me your soda."

Keegan handed over his glass and swung a chair around against the back wall. He said bye with a friendly shove. Aaron dropped his clothes and took his seat, jaw clenched, hands loose.

"Relax, I'm just playing with Keegs." Chase claimed his fresh drink. "What brings you to the dungeons? It wasn't to box, though you surprised us with a good effort."

"Natural athlete, I guess." Aaron downed his whole soda in a few loud gulps. Ember wrapped her fingers around her water, took a larger swallow this time for a reason not to speak.

"Didn't answer my question," Chase reminded with a slow, challenging smile.

"I didn't realize I'd be interrogated."

Their host's eyes narrowed. He angled his body over the table and in front of Ember to illustrate Aaron held his full attention.

"No, you expected to be the only one demanding answers. Fading bouncer."

Ember trembled where she sat, caught between the two teenage alphas, and wondered why she thought this would be a good idea.

Aaron played the game. He returned the stare, slow blinks, but no other movement. Acknowledgement of who was in charge, of whose house he was in. Satisfied, Chase eased back from the table.

"Ember, at least, knows how to answer questions. She said you're looking for your friend, Brandt."

"Last I saw him, he had a run in with Nicu," Aaron said.

"Yeah, I was there."

"What?"

"I was bugging the car in front you."

Aaron's lips twitched, then he laughed. He rested against his chair back and drew a hand through his drying hair.

"Did you stick around for the fallout?" Aaron asked.

"I caught the end." Chase raised his glass and Aaron grabbed his own to toast a prank executed at his expense.

Ember slumped into the booth, scrutinized the pair as if they'd grown new personalities. She crossed her arms, happy to let them hash out their relationship without her, but the movement drew Chase's attention. He drained whatever drink he'd appropriated from Keegan, then slammed the glass to the table.

"So Brandt is your buddy?" Chase asked. Aaron nodded. "Well, I'll be honest, Aaron. The last time you saw him is not the last time I did. See, I caught up with him later. He was piss drunk, spitting mad and had a forearm choke on one of my crew."

Aaron shook his head, gaze downcast. "Keegan?"

"You wish." Chase growled. "Show him."

Ember studied his flush, wondered if this was part of what she owed him. What did it matter if Aaron knew what Brandt had done? He'd stick with his friend against her, so there was no point.

Chase slashed his eyes at her, the demand in them clear. She sat up and lifted her chin.

"Fucking fades." Aaron gulped, his wide stare unable to look away. Not comfortable with the scrutiny, Ember realigned and shifted so her hair fell forward.

"You've been with her all day, yet this is the first time you notice that sucker? Or maybe you didn't consider it important to ask the Trimarked girl where she got hurt? Let me say this, Harwell. I can't help you find your friend, but I can sure as hell tell you Nicu isn't the only one who has reason to toss him off the edge."

Silence for the sake of emphasis.

"Now it's time for you to get out. Ember, you okay taking him home or should I get Keegan?"

Ember peeked beyond the veil of her hair. Aaron sat with his elbows on his knees, his stare wide and apologetic. Ember's stomach churned with his unexpected reaction. Why did she feel like she owed him a favor for caring about her?

"I'll go with Keegan," he offered and turned to grab his shirt. Ember shifted uncomfortably. She understood what Chase's offer meant. He would think if she asked for Keegan's help that Aaron was just like Brandt.

She shook her head, couldn't throw him off the edge when he'd shown her remorse. She spoke quietly around the lump in her throat. "I'll take him. I need to get back to Mom, anyway."

Chase shoved the water into her hands. "Finish that first," he commanded. He was far too aware of her limited resources. Before she could refuse, he rose from the booth and stormed out one of the many doors spaced along the chamber's walls.

12

DEVI

*D*evi Garenne cupped the two-inch quartz in one hand, the other sketched lines and nodes of the spell she'd skimmed from Ember's tattoo. Where Fae focused on the particles of magic and Witches worked with the flow of it, Devi saw the structure of the atoms as if through a microscope. Her eyes fixed on a long run that twisted in the crystal. She drew the line, hash marks to show where it intersected.

"Verge!" She threw her pencil, and it clattered against the concrete floor of the warehouse.

She lost track. Again. Devi gripped the quartz and studied her sketch. The capture had worked. As she brushed the stone against the Ink, the crystals had reshaped and aligned in a copy that was map more than magic. The challenge wasn't her Work, but the tattoo. This spell was so much more complicated than she'd expected.

There was more than Binding Ink within the tattoo's energy. Devi pursed her lips at her drawing, then grabbed a new pencil from the crowded cup on her right and scratched the dark graphite across the ruined sketch in frustration. The crystal was too small. She had trouble following each line past every vertex and through each knot without getting lost in the magnitude.

"I'm glad we found something to stump you." Leona's words drifted into the warehouse before her body. The High Priestess looked around as if not sure how she ended up there. Devi was not fooled for a second. She schooled her face into a calm smile.

"Mother."

Leona's full lips curved up, her fingertips caressed the grain of the table.

"All joking aside, do you think you can do this?" Leona flicked her eyes toward the barrels lined against the wall. Devi flipped a few pages backward in her notebook to the section focused on waste oil, though the project had lost its interest for her with a chance to study Ink.

"In theory, yes. It's separating molecules. The challenge is, they were burned, so returning them to their previous form will not work. I need an idea of what they're likely to turn into, and of what I must manipulate along the way to make sure they won't snap back into their current configuration."

"I'm not sure about the possibility of success here. You are not changing glass to sand."

Devi curled a lip with her mother's dry tone. "I just said as much."

Leona breathed in with careful consideration. Her shoulders shrugged in a graceful curve and she drifted around the table to stand across from Devi.

"Complexity has always been your specialty, I suppose."

"I like puzzles."

Leona chuckled at the understatement.

"Well, if anyone can do it, it is you. It's a shame your unique vision isn't something you can teach."

It wasn't that Devi's methods weren't teachable, but that the other mages were not capable. Ask a dog to view an entire rainbow of colors, or humans to see all the angles a fly experiences and it cannot be done. The other Witches saw flows of energy, rivers and pools, blocks that shifted and stretched. Devi saw strings, the way the energies were tied together to create unique patterns at the caster's command. She could trace them, recreate them, or unravel them by pulling at just the right thread. She had the ability to undo something in a moment, where another Witch might take minutes or hours.

Over time, her success had convinced the coven she could do what she said despite not being able to share it. They had given her intricate spells at an age where other Witches and Wizards were just learning to Work fire. She had charted her own path, chose her own experiments, such as with this project to turn the burnt, dirty oil into something clean and useful.

Yet, with her morning visitor, that task had been brushed aside by magic far more complicated and interesting. Devi rolled the tubular quartz in her palm, then held it to the light in a casual motion, as if her next question wasn't important.

"Can I borrow the scrying stone?"

"For what purpose?"

"To study the intricate components of a spell."

"Are you that close to figuring out this mess?"

Devi dropped the small crystal into her hand. Let her mom think they were still talking about oil. If she knew about the Ink, she might do something horrible, like order Devi to stop studying Fae magic under the belief it was too dangerous for a Witch. "I won't know until I try a few things."

"What will that do to my stone? Will I get it back?"

"Of course you'll get it back."

"Working as it has been?"

"In theory." Devi's smile curved deeper and she widened her eyes as if she could project innocence.

Leona shook her head, not fooled. "Your theories. I grant you your successes, my daughter, but I cannot forget the failures. The scrying stone is important. I need it as is. However, that is not all. You plan to experiment with these spells and I find myself very concerned. You are working with such volatile components."

"Most of the energy has been removed," she countered with a dismissive wave.

Her mother frowned and continued to be unconvinced. Devi considered sharing the truth of why she wanted the crystal ball. She could expand the spell held in her hand within the crystalline structure for more space to dig in and find the weave and weft of Ember's complicated tattoo.

Her hesitation rose from the fact that Witches shouldn't study Fae magic, the threat of mixing powers apparently dangerous. But Devi was sure those rules didn't apply to her. Another point of worry was that even though Fae magic had created the Ink, the Binding used Witch power to help shape the tattoo, not by blending as Leona would worry about, but in collaboration.

To compound the reasons, as Priestess, Leona's involvement with the Trimark was likely. Though she gave her daughter a lot of leeway, Devi wasn't certain how her mother would like having her daughter examine one of her secret projects.

Even if Leona hadn't helped make the Trimark, this magic was used on Ember. That fact more than any other might result in many of Devi's own freedoms trimmed. Acting as High Priestess, Leona could take greater interest in her activities to ensure safety of the coven and distance from the Child.

With twenty years of secrets built up, Devi was not prepared to make such a challenge.

"Is there a reason you came to visit me, then?"

Leona flipped through pages of a text without marking Devi's place. "Do you know why the Trimarked brought a human here?"

"I didn't meet a human."

"No. I did, while you met with her."

"It did not come up in our conversation." Devi rescued her

book, placed a flower petal where she needed it.

Leona hummed. "He was looking for someone, thought I would scry for him with the very stone you're requesting to borrow."

Devi's dark red brow rose in response. "I assume he got the same answer I did."

"Of course not." Leona's smile indicated he had not gotten his way, either. "Granted, I never answered. Instead, we took a walk through the greenhouse and mixed a basic friendship charm."

"That is not like you." In fact, her mother was very adamant magic should not be Worked on humans. The only spells she wanted humans to see were the kind that kept the coven useful, such as earth and water magic for growing things. By showing the humans the Witches' ability to care for household yards, they were more likely to barter for the fruits and vegetables grown along the banks of the river.

"I'm not inclined to cast spells for all humans as our ancestors had, no. I'm in no hurry to start another round of Witch hunts, especially when we have nowhere to run. He only got my consideration because he came with the Child."

Leona's lips thinned. She jerked away from the table, movements stiff and sharp. "Well, it can't be helped. At least it was a simple charm and a show for just one boy. What is of interest, why did the Trimarked need you? Something that led you to request the scrying stone right after her human friend asked about it seems a bit more than coincidence."

"Ember doesn't care about the oil," Devi deflected.

"No, but you turned three or four pages back from where you were when I arrived. It makes me think you may have multiple projects."

High Priestess for a reason, Leona's flighty persona often misled people into thinking she was simple. Even though she might not understand what Devi wrote into her books, she clearly paid attention to other details.

Before Devi could devise another misdirect, a small runner around eight years old burst into the warehouse, the lines on his face smoothing with the sight of the High Priestess.

"Nicu Coccia is requesting an escort while he inspects the barrier."

"Interesting and unexpected." Leona hummed, her posture aligned. "What is his location now?"

"He's waiting at the human corner."

"I wonder if he'll be forthcoming in why he really wants to enter our territory, or if he'll be as irritating as usual," Leona mused. "I need to send someone who can deal with their evasions."

Devi stared at the quartz in her hand, peered deep at the perplexing ties inside. She didn't have a bigger crystal, but if she had something similar to compare the patterns to, something simpler, she might be able to sort it out. The idea grew, urged her to stand and search her table for another palm-length stone.

"I'll go," she offered as soon as she had hands on the quartz, this one octagonal rather than tubular, but the effect within would be the same.

"To babysit a Fae?" Leona asked.

And to get away from her mom's prying eyes.

"Yes. I need a break. Might as well have fun irritating Nicu."

Devi broke into the sunshine. She cut across the Circle with powerful legs used to chewing up distance and dodged whatever she found in her path, much to the startled cries of a few coven members. Her heartbeat quickened, her face flushed, and she worked to calm herself down.

It wouldn't do any good to let Nicu see her excitement, not when she intended to leverage what she needed to learn about Ember's Binding Ink to get something else she'd always wanted — a chance to study the Living Ink, too.

13

NICU

*N*icu checked the barrier along Fae lands, first. The energy within Trifecta shifted with each territory. The power of his people lined up as if drawn by magnetic forces, curved and straightened with each form of Nature, or as the Fae molded and structured it.

From there, he moved to the human neighborhood. The power here dug deep into every aspect of the landscape as if in hiding, so it was difficult to grasp.

Witch land had energy that swirled and bent as fickle as the breeze, and eager to be harnessed. As he neared their border, that power reached out to him in the form of a wind-arrow that struck his shoulder in warning and greeting. Had he continued or declared himself an enemy, that same air could be narrowed into a much thinner and deadlier stream. As it was, he planted his feet, stated his cause, and settled in to wait.

The Law of Convergence ensured all races had access to the whole of Trifecta. The agreement to allow humans to wander had been an acknowledgement of this being their realm first, and just because the Fade forced new residents in did not mean they lost land rights within it. In the end, the humans chose segregation for themselves, anyway.

Between the mages of Fae and Witch, however, this agreement was not valid. They reverted to the rules of true realm travel. No entry without invitation. No ambassadors had free passage. Visitors always under guard, the reason Nicu waited for an escort. With her arrival, the threatening magic around him eased, but the tension in Nicu's shoulders did not.

"Devi." The word was not a greeting.

"I came to see for myself. What have you done, Nicu Coccia, for your council of Elders to give you such a pointless task?"

"Perhaps you don't understand the importance."

Devi's eyes flashed, but her lips curled.

"Is this about the Ternate? Are you hoping for chaos to knock down the wall?" she asked.

"May I proceed?"

Devi looked between him, the patrol Witches, and the invisible barricade. "Well, come along then. I don't have all day."

Nicu broke the boundary with his foot, now on Witch land, surrounded by Witch magic. He kept his fingertips against the solid surface of the Veil's bubble, tested the bond and flow of power in search for chinks or pockets. He never used, never manipulated, simply read.

Devi snorted. "Fae, treating magic like a cookbook you never intend to use."

"Witches, treating magic as if it were a plaything."

"An element," she challenged.

"Forgetting consequences."

"You force others to pay the price when you need an excuse to bend it to your will."

"Old covenants best left in the past."

The Fae had once encouraged humans, had since learned even with someone else paying, the use of High Magic proved too costly. Witches were not able to grasp time or space manipulation, did not understand the consequences of the power commanded by Fate. Gifted as Devi appeared to be, those magics would be beyond her, so this pointless conversation was intended as a deflection. Nicu stiffened his guard.

They came across a stretch of jutted cliff face and the elevation broke Nicu's contact. He studied the craggy surface for a minute, then reached.

"You're seriously going to climb that? The Fae haven't been this interested in the barrier since its appearance."

Nicu ignored her and climbed, searched out hand and footholds with sight and touch, kept close to the edge and tested the energy every few feet, as he made sure nothing had changed. These areas were considered impenetrable, not only because of the barrier, but also geography, which made it a prime location for an attempted break.

Devi and her one visible scout followed the gradual incline as he crossed the cliff face until the elevation and bluff converged. Feet back on the ground, a hard breath out, Nicu brushed dust and pebbles from his sweater.

"All right, Nicu, I admit that was impressive. And here you didn't even break a sweat."

Devi brushed over his forearms as if testing the dampness of his skin. Hidden between thumb and palm, he felt the cool gem touch first. Her fingers followed and dragged a flow of power. He twisted back a step, body tense in defense.

The scout's bow raised, focused on Nicu even though Devi had offended. The Witch wrapped her hand around the crystal, still unseen, and tucked it into her pocket.

"Ember saw me this morning." Devi's warning to let it go, a signal to not alert the mages watching.

He would play.

"Why did she visit a Witch?"

"There are questions we cannot ask directly. It's rarely certain why she visits."

Nicu stepped back, accepted the Witch's veiled apology,

and debated the words needed to keep the surface conversation light while the true meaning prevailed.

"If you discover it is important, you will tell me."

Devi's smile was full of teeth.

"All in the spirit of coexistence. I assume you would do the same."

Nicu twisted his wrist against the ghost chill of the gem. He wondered what Devi searched for, and wanted to know how it pertained to Ember.

He returned to checking the barrier, questions unasked. Currently, Ember remained controlled. He tolerated Devi's curiosity for the moment, and would remember to follow up.

"All is well, then?" Devi asked as they bordered Fae land at the end of the sweep.

"The barrier is as expected. Your cooperation is appreciated."

Nicu's eyes flickered toward Devi's pocket. She marked the movement and nodded in reply. Satisfied, Nicu stepped once more into Fae territory, back into the patterns of aligned magic, full circle.

Now to visit the anomaly.

No Man's Land, the true center of Trifecta, where Fae, Witch and human energies negated each other, repelled magic and nature, and created a neutral zone. Nothing grew here. Animals avoided the space. Trees had fallen years ago, possibly at the point the barrier appeared. Grass had died and entropy ruled.

Nicu's lungs worked hard to bring in stale air. His feet sunk deep into the mass of decay. He crouched and sifted through the brown pine needles, leaves and organic material on the forest floor, the energy heavy with lack of life. Even the sounds of the inhabited forest around him were blocked from the clearing.

He lifted his hand, sprinkled debris and watched it fall

without interference. No breeze, no flutter, just simple gravity drawing the pieces back to earth.

Nothing had been through here. The only disturbances were his own divots in an otherwise plush area of decay. Yet....

Something tugged at him, a belief in his gut indicating not all was as it seemed. The silence distracted him, his discomfort overshadowed what caused his foreboding.

After long moments, Nicu stood. The dome proved unmolested upon inspection. No Man's Land was undisturbed. Now he needed to see if he could find the fragments of barrier energy Branna had noticed. He turned toward the Trimarked Child's home.

The returned breeze announced the shift from No Man's to human land. Squirrels hustled between trees, sought the perfect secret place to bury their nuts. Birds called to each other, their songs urgent with the turning of the seasons upon them. Nicu absorbed the sounds, let them roll through him as he loped in a random zig zag, careful never to create a trail despite the many times he'd made his way to the same spot.

From a few trees deep, Nicu examined the dilapidated yard surrounding the concrete structure the Lees called home. From the shadows, he searched for energies different from what should exist. His senses skimmed the area, tripped over an anomaly, but could not grasp anything solid. He advanced, narrowed his eyes in concentration, held his breath in frustration.

What did he sense? Was it Veil energy?

He couldn't tell other than it was outside the natural streams of power within human lands. He had to get closer.

The door on the side of the hybrid girl's dwelling opened. Instinct sent him back into camouflage. Practice kept him hidden against Ember's habitual scan of the terrain before she turned to someone else leaving the tunnel.

Aaron Harwell emerged from the staircase. Nicu straightened from his tree, eyes strained in focus, one ear tilted forward to catch any sound.

Hunched shoulders, Harwell's hands sat deep in his jacket pockets, his face downcast. Ember's entire form stiffened as he continued to speak to her, to approach her. Nicu's breath stopped. His blood slowed to keep him rooted where he hid, and he waited for a sign she might need him.

He remained motionless, patient, controlled, until the moment he saw something he could never unsee that brought an unexpected, unwelcome end to Nicu's sense of security.

14

EMBER

*E*mber matched Aaron's reluctant pace. He scuffed his toes in the dust and pain outlined his face, clear even in the tunnel's gloom.

Ember swallowed and averted her eyes, tried to remember she didn't care what this human boy thought or felt.

"He did that to you?" The constriction in his words cut through her, and she jerked out a nod. "Fade, Ember, I'm so sorry."

"Not your fault. No reason to apologize."

"If I hadn't let Brandt go off half-cocked, or if I'd kept him at the party.... I guess Nicu doesn't babysit you."

Ember choked out a pained laugh and stopped her steps, turned her back to Aaron and pressed her palms over her cheeks.

"It was nice to see you have friends, though." There he went, taking it one step further.

"Nicu is not my friend."

"No, I meant Chase."

Ember faced him, her brow furrowed. "You have the wrong idea. Chase and I have a business relationship. Right now I am in his debt."

"Is that why you didn't finish the water he gave you?"

Ember shrugged against the tension in her neck. The hair on her arms raised as an uncomfortable buzz crawled over her skin. Aaron saw too much. That meant she should get him out of here, send him home, away from her as fast as possible.

At the exit, Ember threw her weight into the bar and thrust it open. She took the time to scan the hillside despite her agitation before she let Aaron follow.

"Will you forgive me?" he asked.

The handle slipped out of Ember's grip and the door slammed.

"What?"

"For Brandt. For not stopping him last night. Forgive me?"

Bile burned Ember's tongue. She looked toward the forest, uncertain of how to act.

"What if I said I need you to?"

Ember jerked her attention to the impossible boy before her. He took it as an invitation to step closer, curled his shoulders to draw in his height and leaned forward.

Ember's stomach twisted. She angled away from him, not understanding what his game was.

"I can't help you find Brandt."

"I know." Aaron stood still, his eyes danced across her features.

"Go home, Aaron."

"I need you to."

Ember moved backward. The icy steel door blocked her escape.

"Ember, I—" He closed the distance between them. Ember raised her hands to ward him off, stomach sucked in on an inhale. Aaron's hand gripped her wrist.

Power slipped between their skin, separated his touch from hers with a hard, invisible shield. Dust flew up around them in an artificial burst of wind. Dirt struck Aaron's eyes, pressured him to move away.

He threw up an arm, letting her go. Air settled back into stagnant movement, the only sounds were their heavy breathing. Blue light sparked between spread fingers and drew both their attention to the beautiful death sentence.

Ember trembled, her entire body primed for fight or flight.

Except she couldn't run. He might tell someone.

Except she couldn't fight. She might give herself away and make Aaron aware of her ability to open the barrier.

"Verge," she choked. The door supported her. Aaron shifted to block anyone's view from the street, open palms out at his sides, a helpless gesture as he stared at the uncontrolled power.

"What do I do?"

Leave me alone! Ember wanted to scream the words, to hit him with the pent up pressure caught behind her ribs. The visible energy flattened, spread up her arms and caressed every bit of her body. Tears pooled in her eyes as she watched the movement. Her skin was covered in the same impenetrable magic of the barrier, power that glowed pale blue with painless flickers. Painless, but not harmless.

Ember lowered her head in forlorn denial, kept her hands out as if to push the magic and the truth away from herself. A thick well of moisture fell, saturated by blue-tinged energy as it left the curve of her cheek in descent.

Swift, warm air scented with pine and mist pressed against Ember's side. A long forearm covered in curved tattoos slipped under hers and caught the single tear in mid-fall.

Tension eased, became the weight of understanding. Acceptance.

"She is not attacking me."

Aaron doing what? Defending? It wouldn't do any good, but how would the golden boy understand what this meant?

Heaviness too strong to fight kept her neck bowed. She lifted her eyes toward her fate, to receive Nicu and through him, the Fae. Her attention caught with morbid fascination on his fingertips as they darkened with the movement of his tattoos.

Magic pumped in pin-prick rivulets through her body with each pass of Nicu's thumb over his fingers, her heart beat in time. The ripples condensed at her chest, flowed along the length of her arms and pooled in the spaces between her fingers to condense into a dancing blue web of electrical flashes. The power sparked into the air, drops rose to the sky, rain in reverse.

Lightning danced between the clouds and thunder rumbled a quiet, deep threat.

Ember flexed her fingers, checked to see they weren't shaking or glowing, not believing it had been that easy. Dissipated because of Nicu.

In debt to Nicu.

She tucked her hands behind her back and lowered her lashes.

"See, under control," Aaron announced, unaware Ember had nothing to do with the fix.

"She's leaking."

"Um, you know what tears are, don't you? Or do Fae not cry?"

"Always so reckless, little hybrid."

Ember's eyes snapped open at his challenge. She sucked in a deep breath to forget how tired she was. Straightened her spine to chase away the fear. She pulled forth aggravations. Every time he followed her, how he showed up to keep others from her so she remained segregated, and each stupid time she'd wanted him to interfere, and he hadn't.

Nicu leaned back to give her room. The tension left his face as the fervor returned to hers and anger flushed her skin. He did not dare bring out the fight in her if all he meant to do was punish her for possessing power she had not chosen.

Then he noticed her throat, and he stilled.

"Who hurt you?"

Oh, verge, the bruise from Brandt that led to more proof of her ability. Ember's eyes flickered to Aaron in alarm. Nicu took it as an answer.

As if Nicu were the only one who could move, he turned on Aaron. One hand flattened against the human's collar bone, propelled him onto the brick, fingers slid up his neck to mirror the bruise Ember wore.

Aaron's face flushed with the effort to try escape. He struggled for leverage and kicked forward. Nicu twisted aside while refusing Aaron's shoulders an inch of movement.

"Nicu, no! It was Brandt," Ember said.

Nicu glanced toward her, read the truth in that brief contact, then narrowed his attention on Aaron without offering release.

"Where is your friend?"

Aaron paled. "You don't know?"

"It is not my habit to keep track of gulls."

"H-he disappeared. After last night, I thought you—"

Nicu shoved himself away from Aaron, thrusting the boy against the brick with his momentum. The breadth of Nicu's body yawned over Ember. She met him with her chin raised. They stood, a battle of silent wills.

"You always inflict complication. You have called too much attention to yourself."

"No one needs to know." Aaron hadn't moved except to lean his head back. "It's just the three of us."

"Three is a larger number than zero." Nicu's logic shattered a moment of hope. "There is nothing we can do to hide what she is."

"Who she is," Aaron corrected.

"No, what," Ember agreed. "Trimarked."

Nicu nodded, eased away when he realized she understood. "I have tried to tell you, little hybrid. People look. And now you have gotten caught." Nicu's attention flickered along the length of her tense form before returning to study her face.

"What's next?" Her breath was a whisper. Nicu shook his head.

"A battle of duty."

"What does that mean?" Aaron demanded. Nicu shifted between the human and Ember, his back to the boy.

"Consequences will come. You have removed all chance of keeping them at bay. Get inside and stay."

Nicu maneuvered around her and retreated to the forest.

Ember never took her eyes from Nicu, not convinced he left, or that her only repercussion was to be sent home. For now.

"He's an ass." Aaron broke the silence as he wrenched himself from the wall.

Nicu, gone. He'd just walked away as usual. As if their interaction had been normal.

Somehow, that made everything worse.

"Go home, Aaron." She flinched when she realized she echoed Nicu, passed by Aaron without another word because she still meant what she said.

"Wait. Em!" Ember paused at the corner of the building. "Thank you for letting me hang out today. Especially since I had been looking for the guy who hurt you."

How was he so damned nice? Ember studied Aaron's tall form, the way the wind tugged at his tight curls, his hands back in his jacket against the afternoon chill. Suddenly, she couldn't handle the weight he'd placed on her shoulders, or the demand his presence made. So she let him go.

"Yes."

Aaron frowned. "Yes, what?"

"To your question earlier. Yes."

Aaron's smile was white and brilliant when he fit the pieces together, realizing she meant she forgave him.

"Thank you, Em. That means the world to me."

With that, Aaron Harwell jogged away.

15

DEVI

*D*evi rested in a deep squat, not interested in sitting on the damp floor of the small cave. Eyes closed, hands in prayer to support the pose rather than in supplication. Devi sent her desires into the dense air and waited.

The tubular cave must have been an underground river long ago, feeding into the Pine River at the place Devi had found its entrance. A heavy fall of fat roots and twisted vines made the opening difficult to find, and no one else had discovered it while playing with a childhood imaginary friend.

She never spoke about the cave, though not with any purposeful intention to keep it secret. This place was just hers. It drew her in through the tangled foliage, to a clean and unadorned passage. Rock walls clear of moss or the penetration of roots led her down the hollow, dead end track with no turn offs, no fear of getting lost in a maze. The deepest part of the cave widened by a few feet, the naked stone ceiling rose by the same to create a cavern saturated with magic.

The chamber sat directly under No Man's Land, and other than lacking signs of life, they existed as opposites. She only came when she needed to, though not with reluctance. She always left as soon as she finished, though not in a hurry. This place did not exactly feel safe, while being incredibly alluring, immersed as it was by power and knowledge.

Today she studied crystal growth. The smallest molecule multiplying into a larger, glass-like creation. How they bound together, suspended in space, how she could manipulate them to grow, expand and never lose their essence or shape. The size of her quartz crystals did not matter. As long as Devi kept their connections intact, their physical nature could be what she willed.

Insight rippled through her, generated a minor ache with the effort, and she stood. With each step toward the outside world, Devi rolled her shoulders and tilted her neck, eased off layers of gravid power and left nothing behind but gratitude.

The downward sun marked how late the day had become. Devi ran her tongue across the tips of her teeth. She debated her need to get back to the Circle and try out her new theory, but turned in the opposite direction instead to a space between No Man's Land and the main road.

Chase Casterline leaned against a privacy fence that marked the edge of the first occupied human house off the Witch border. The small velvet bag he tossed between his hands clinked as the stones within crashed against each other.

"You're late."

Devi raised a brow. "I don't have to be here."

"It isn't a problem," Chase continued as if she hadn't spoken. "I just got here myself. Business matters."

"I wasn't going to come at all. I can't stay today."

"Then why show up? I wouldn't care."

As odd as it sounded to Devi, she knew he meant it. He'd even return in case she showed for the next scheduled meet. The peculiarity of one promised nothing, who had to work for everything, she supposed.

"Ember is having trouble with someone."

"A human," Chase said.

"No."

"I wasn't asking."

Devi frowned, remembered her mom had said something about a tagalong this morning.

"Then she has two problems," Devi said.

"Could it be the same issue with many players?"

"I doubt it when one of them is Fae."

"Who's counting complications when it comes to the Trimarked girl? The Fae problem is Nicu, I suppose."

"Edan." The corner of Devi's lips tilted up when Chase's thick brows sunk to darken his eyes. "As amusing as it is to know something you don't, I assume this happened sometime last night. You were with her, right? What did you notice?"

Chase's features smoothed in an instant. He pulled his hood up.

"Let me get back to you on that."

"Having multiple masters must be a real pain," Devi snapped.

"Drop it, Devi," Chase said. His long strides carried him toward an odd triangular structure that sat close to the street. One of the many scattered entrances to the underground, this one was only large enough for the drop of a staircase.

"Of all your deals, Chase, I'm the only one who will help you learn spells." The words hissed between them. She had no way of knowing if they were alone or if someone listened from the other side of the fence. Her threat worked, stopped Chase in his tracks and made him turn to face her again.

"And as you hold those cards, I hope you'd understand I would not insult you. Even with multiple masters, as you call them, I don't always have the entire picture. Besides, didn't you say you can't stay?"

Devi's fists clenched. Her shoulders wound so tight they reached her ears. She wanted to go home, to get something to eat after half a day away, to pull out the crystals in her pockets and study their secrets. She had a point to prove, though.

To be honest, it wasn't his lack of answer that bothered her.

"Fine," she said through rigid lips. "You can contact me if you need to meet earlier."

Chase's parting head bob might have been part of his natural movement. She let him go, watched him pass through the door down to his underground world. Her shoulders relaxed because this time she'd given him permission.

16

EMBER

*E*mber imagined multiple escape plans, weighing each one against its chance for success. Nicu would return, but she didn't have to follow his orders. She could try to save herself. She should attempt to get herself through the barrier again, with this sudden flush of power. And if not, maybe Chase knew of a deep dark cave where she could hide.

Her eyes dropped as if the frayed toes of her canvas shoes might direct her toward a favorable outcome. She dragged her feet forward, studied them, too tired to acknowledge the futile nature of her search.

The shoes didn't save her. A grim shadow slipped around the corner, leaned his heavy shoulder against the exterior of her house. Ember froze and felt an unintended prickle of power at the base of her spine.

"Ember Lee." Edan nodded his head the smallest fraction as if this were a planned meeting of friends. "I need you to get me out of Trifecta."

Ember walked away. She wanted to run inside, turn the lock and end this strange day.

"I also want you to let me back in."

Right. Ember stopped, struggled to close her mouth against

a useless threat. She looked over the yard and blinked through an attempt to order her thoughts. The hill sloped to the road. The thick tree line hid the next row of houses. Beyond that, more immovable trees, more invisible houses. As the sky darkened to purple, bright autumn colors faded in an attempt to match the rich evergreen shades.

Making a deal with a Fae would be like that, one thing on the surface hiding a multitude of meanings. Ember spent all day preparing or running from this, forgetting it at the moment she'd lost control of a power she didn't want. Yet, here Edan stood, wanting something so easy, and so terrifying.

What had Devi told her? Speak in absolutes. Edan had begun, so were they negotiating now? He'd said two sentences. Did that mean one item, a round trip, or was it separate agreements?

Either way, she had to talk or the debate might finish before she weighed in.

"I don't understand." Ember winced, aware she was already behind in this game.

"I need out, then back in."

"Out, then right back in?" Her brow wrinkled, Devi's voice in the back of her mind shouting at her. Why ask for help if you're not going to use it?

Fades, it had been a long day if Devi was the voice of reason inside her head.

"No." Edan frowned and moved to stand beside her. "I'll return whenever I complete my task. I don't know how long."

Okay, she could add to that.

"I've never done it in reverse."

Edan studied the sun as it lowered toward the top of the trees, the orange blaze suffocating under blankets of violet and blue. Ember's stomach spasmed with nerves.

"Is this a real Fae negotiation? Since you said nothing back, did we decide on something?"

Edan's lips quirked in an actual smile, one he directed at

her in this upside-down world where Nicu let her get away with a major offense and she amused Edan.

"As you are not Fae, I have suspended my expectations for this conversation."

"Oh." Good to know. Ember rested against the wall while vertigo passed.

"The risk is acceptable."

"What risk is that?" The only risk Ember saw was her own chance of getting caught if she helped.

"The risk of not being able to return."

"I—"

Opening the barrier to let humans out was one thing, especially those from underground. Nobody noticed them. Throwing Brandt out, a human with friends, had caused an immense headache. Sending a Fae on his way would certainly be detected, and she had enough trouble to drown in.

"Is something that wrong?" Her whispered question floated between them.

"If it is, my departure would likely benefit you as well."

Logic hard to argue with. Ember looked at her hands, remembered them flashing blue, and shook her head. She didn't want to help him, and she even had a reason he must accept.

"Nicu told me to stay home."

"You seldom listen."

Ember tapped her fingers on her thighs for two beats before curling them into fists. "I will this time."

"Because I made this request?" Edan's cheeks darkened. His weight shifted to hover over her.

"You didn't see?"

Edan's eyes flickered over her face, her hands, along the building as if he could see around the corner and discover what happened minutes into recent history. His head tilted, gathered bits of sound from his memory and echoes from the passing wind.

"And then Nicu told you to stay. It is serious, then." And he left.

Ember gaped at his quick departure, wondered how he suddenly knew without actually knowing. At least the result ended in her favor.

How in convergence had she gotten herself into this — these situations?

How was she going to get out of them?

Ember pulled the crisp air deep into her lungs and the chill took over the heat of adrenalin. She rubbed her arms and figured she might as well think where it was warm.

She turned the knob and walked into the dim room. A different panic squeezed her chest when she didn't see her mom on the couch. When she found Susan in the kitchen, humming and making dinner from the food Ember had brought the night before, she froze.

"Get inside, it's cold out there." Like a normal mom to an ordinary girl, admonished with a smile. Susan's messy hair had been redone, smooth against her scalp and twisted into a neat bun. Pajamas and afghan were replaced with comfortable leggings, a baggy blouse and long cardigan.

Ember closed the door with a soft click, afraid if she shut out the evening the magic would disappear.

"Are you hungry?"

Not spell, then. A reprieve. Ember's chest expanded, her face flushed.

This was horrible timing.

The last thing Ember wanted to do was eat and hang out. Her carefully maintained existence had torn at the seams, left her disoriented with no clear direction and few chances for help. She needed to put cold water on her face. She craved slipping into her tiny, dark bedroom and crawling into bed, to cool her overworked brain and ease her stumbling heartbeat. To plan before she ran.

She wrestled with her thoughts, refused to accept her first reaction.

Her mom was up. A visage of the woman from back when Susan tried to pretend they might be normal. A pretense that ended when Ember was no longer welcome at school, when Susan was faced with the truth every day, and every day she'd given more of her time to the couch than to her daughter.

"Y-yeah." Ember took a deep breath and forced a smile. If her life was falling apart, why not have one evening where she dove into the dream. "That sounds great."

"Perfect. Will you set the table, please?"

With slow movements, Ember did as she was asked, careful to keep her secrets from her fragile parent. She wasn't certain why Susan's mind provided this reprieve, but was grateful for it.

Ember let go of her hell of a day, focused on each smile, on each joke flung her way, enjoyed every moment with this version of her mom. She remembered a happier, if nervous mother, stories told at bedtime of princesses who saved kingdoms. Dinner was reminiscent of a quieter time, a moment when she'd been blind to her Trimark, ignorant to what her existence meant. Remembering innocence was painful. Not taking part would be devastating.

The ending came quietly. Susan's eyes drooped, her smile slackened. They cleaned up together until Susan's fingers trembled. Ember caught the cup as it slipped from her mom's grip, then eased Susan back to bed and tucked her in, a gentle kiss on her cheek. Ember finished the dishes and left the lights on in case Susan woke up in the middle of the night, the light an anchor to dreams that often followed the older woman after waking.

Ensconced in her room, Ember slipped off her shoes, made a hoodie into a pillow and withdrew into thoughts, back to the two Fae who played with her fate.

If what Edan said was true, if his leaving was important, Nicu would send him first.

Then, Nicu. His choice to walk away hadn't fooled Ember. Nicu would always be around for protection or punishment. He presented an odd source of consistency, not in any way a comfort considering the depth of the threat. With the heaviness of nausea, she found she didn't want to leave the only constant she had, even if she could use her powers for herself. No one was as reliable, including her mom.

Nicu provided something else, though. A desire to fight.

She'd always fought against the restrictions Nicu placed on her. She'd always thought she'd been fighting him, and through him, the Fae.

But he'd dispersed her power today. He'd given warnings instead of rebukes. He hadn't dragged her to the Fae. Instead, he'd walked away, and she couldn't ignore that. Couldn't sleep because of it.

Nicu was still Fae. He still held too much power over her head. Yet, today, he'd given her something new, something very not-Fae, and something she had so little of.

He'd given her a choice. To stay, or to run.

Resolve sank into her bones. She would not give in.

Now she had to figure out what not giving in looked like.

17

BRANDT

*B*randt huddled under the branches of a pine, breathed into his hands and tried to filter out the overpowering scent of evergreen. Twenty-four hours gone and nothing to show for it.

He'd gotten away from the jerks who'd grabbed him. Brandt didn't want to be followed and figured the woods to be safer, so he'd run through the forest, though it required detours around boulders and scrambling over steep drops.

At some point he made a choice to head toward the city, a place where there should be help. As the terrain leveled out and he rejoined the road, he'd slowed to a halt. His chest heaved, not from effort, but from the realization that those lights were further than he imagined.

"Verge!" The shout faded into the silence, sending a shiver along Brandt's spine when he had to acknowledge just how alone he was.

A few more yards away, he noticed a bulky, pipe-welded gate across the very road that wound up to Trifecta. Why was it blocked? Was this why no one visited anymore? The bubble dropped and the entire world left them be? He circled the bars, stomach twisted with acid, and read the yellow sign bolted to its front.

Warning: Road Closed Due to Landslide

Brandt looked back up the mountain. Trifecta wasn't visible because of the incline and the close pressed trees. Could there have been an avalanche?

He set a sedate pace, not just because of the slope but because he was less interested in the return trip. The road's edges crumbled to the dirt shoulder, the center solid with sun bleached dividing lines. Nothing. No washout, no landslide, not even a felled tree stopped his progress.

What in the realms? He knew nobody from Trifecta placed that sign, at least not physically. Only one answer made sense. Magic.

Magic got them stuck. Mages didn't fix it. Trimarked powers kicked him out. In fact, the more time he spent outside, the clearer his mind became, like a veil lifted from thoughts he'd always had, but wasn't allowed to think. It became easier to see living in a bubble was no way to live. Magic did not belong in a human world, not if it created bubbles that locked people up. Not if it made them exist together as if they were a peaceful, if disjointed family. How had that happened, anyway? How had the humans of Trifecta stepped aside without a fight, giving up so much of their space, so much of their lives?

Why the hell did Ember keep them there, knowing she could get them out? Then again, she was fading Trimarked. Magic stuck with magic.

Nothing he could do about that, though, and all that running left him starved.

The city too far away, he supposed it best to stick it out at the edges of Trifecta, at least for another night. He'd snuck into camp while the guys who lived there were on patrol, looking for anyone else who fell off, probably. He should have grabbed a blanket, but he hadn't wanted to get caught again. With an armful of food, he'd gotten right back out and searched until he found a cozy spot under a tree with low-hanging boughs where he took cover and fumed in peace.

No joke, he'd been waiting to escape that bubble his entire life. There weren't a lot of places in a ten mile diameter to hide from the fists of his old man. There were too many people stuck following their desperate need to live normal, pretending to be ordinary. The few who looked beyond themselves didn't know what to do with a kid who played hard, fought harder, yet still had a few more bruises than could be explained.

Aaron was looking for him in all the usual places, he was sure. Solid Aaron always found him. Of course, today he wouldn't. Aaron would spin himself into a tizzy. He probably assumed Brandt was playing a prank after the 'she's not worth it' crap the soccer captain had pulled last night. Granted, it was something Brandt would do. He bit back a laugh, choked it down behind a bite of food and listened to the forest to figure out if anyone heard him. Shit, he had to remember to be quiet, now.

The worst part of all this, Brandt had been convinced he'd break that invisible shield one day, like a gigantic glass dome. Reporters would line up to interview Trifecta's hero. With enough fame and fortune, it would be possible to leave his dad behind and start an actual life. He never thought he'd be kicked out because of a secret. And what a massive, fading secret that girl had. A secret that might help their stupid town, open them to the rest of the world.

Instead, she kept to herself, enjoyed the power for herself, and got to be the entire town's damn jailor. No wonder she was so damned cocky. If the barrier hadn't been older than them, he might even think she'd been responsible for the entire fading thing.

The temperature dropped with the sun and Brandt pulled his knees into his chest to stay warm. Sure, he could return to that stupid camp with their fires and blankets, but those guys were in on it, grabbed him right away, took him out and far from the party so he didn't run up to his friends and shout out what that mutt had done. It was a surprise he'd gotten any food from them, actually, but good to know since he would need to go back tomorrow.

Exhaustion settled over Brandt, weighed his head so it dipped toward his knees.

Dry wood snapped. Brandt jerked. Still heavy with sleep, he sunk into himself. The tree shivered around his body, shocked him wide awake, muscles flushed with adrenalin.

Branches creaked and parted as if on hinges. In the gap, Brandt made out a black shadow too tall for a mountain cat, too thin to be a bear. Then, with a snap of the stranger's fingers, fire appeared between them. The long, narrow stretch of a man lowered, folded like a piece of origami shifting from one form to another until he crouched level with Brandt. An ankle-length, open coat with thick lapels pooled on the ground. The curves and dips of a trilby hat held back his cinnamon-colored hair. The flame he cupped in his hand brightened green gem-tone eyes.

"Gn-gnome," Brandt stuttered, pressed against the trunk behind him. The man tsked in reply.

"Such language toward a potential friend."

Brandt's lips curled. "You're not my type."

The man laughed into the night.

"I would say the same, but it seems we have similar goals."

"To kick some girl's ass?"

Sharp features froze around a stiff smile.

"A girl? I was thinking a little bigger, but big plans require baby steps. Come with me to get something to eat. We can talk about proposals on the way."

Going with this guy meant he wouldn't need to steal from the forest patrol's camp the next day, or risk death by exposure trying to reach that city that might be days of walking away.

On the other hand, the guard guys were human, easy enough to sneak around. This dude was a Wizard.

"Who are you?" Brandt demanded.

"My name is Tristan." The calm answer only set Brandt more on edge.

"How did you find me?"

"I've watched you since your... expulsion yesterday. Quite a field trip you went on. I assume you found out Trifecta is separated by more than just a bubble?"

Brandt remained silent. This mage had tracked him all day? Not if the polished tops of his shoes told the truth. Brandt was covered in sweat and dirt, himself.

Tristan sighed. "I see the distrust in your eyes and I suppose it's warranted. However, remember this, young human. Magic got you out. How do you think you'll get back in?"

Brandt released some tension.

"You can do that?"

"A tricky question that ultimately ends in a yes."

"What if I don't want to go back? What if I prefer to head to the city?"

"Then you'll never get your revenge. Although, that would need to wait until our deal is completed. If you agree to help me." Tristan unfolded and stepped back to make the gap in tree branches wider.

"But I don't have to?"

"You are a person of choice." An odd way to answer, but Brandt went with it. At this point, his stomach was trying to strangle him for not taking the gnome up on his offer of food.

"Okay. Yeah." Brandt pushed himself up, cramped muscles slowed him. He brushed prickly twigs and damp earth from his jeans as he walked through the space Tristan made. He glanced at the Wizard, took in his narrow height, almost a head above Brandt who was already six three. Brandt had a few pounds more of muscle and fewer years, though, so he liked his chances.

Once out, the branches sprang back into position, the breeze they created propelled him to follow the man with the flame.

"Do you know why the barrier exists?"

"Something about realms competing to be in the same place," Brandt grumbled with a shrug. "What does that have to do with anything?"

"The goal was to create a passageway, right here, between the realms. Instead, the Veil fought back, and the pathway turned into a trap." Tristan paused, looked over his shoulder as if waiting for Brandt to participate.

"Mages, then. Humans would have done it right."

The Wizard's sigh sounded like a disappointed teacher's. "Please follow along. This is important. I can get you inside. You will owe me a favor."

"So tell me what to do. I don't need a history lesson. Unless you were the one who caused it." Brandt's last words burst out on a rush of angry fear just as they brushed across his thoughts. He swallowed hard, as if he might take them back in case this guy became pissed.

"Current events," the man corrected with a scowl. "And no, I did not cause it, but it's important knowledge to have. You must know the nature of something before you can change it." He stopped and stepped aside. Brandt crashed into an invisible wall. At some point, they'd left the forest for the road, too. Brandt swiped at his nose and turned to glare at the Wizard, but got sidetracked when he saw the Now Leaving Trifecta sign.

"W-what? How did we get here so fast?"

"I'm good at making paths, more evidence to show I did not botch this up to create a bubble in the Veil. Now, listen carefully." Tristan hinged forward, flame held to the side of their faces. "You were born in Trifecta. Your blood has a unique connection to it I can use. I will return you, and you will bring me the one connected to the barrier."

"I have business with her, too, but you'll have her."

Unblinking emeralds studied Brandt's face, weighed his words, analyzed his whole damn worth. Brandt shifted between his feet, uncomfortable under the gaze.

"She has information I need. I insist our agreement takes precedent."

"Yeah, I get it." Brandt paced away from the man, turned when he felt he'd reached a safe enough distance to glower back, and copied the guy's infuriating tone. "We both want the bitch who can open the barrier. But I can't get her until I am in there." Brandt slapped his palm to the flat air beside him.

With a shrug, Tristan walked forward and slipped a Bowie knife from a pocket inside his coat. The blade was thick and long, sharp along one length, then a slight curve up the backside, and it had a channel through each side of the middle. The Wizard grabbed Brandt's hand from where it illustrated Trifecta's outer boundary. A whispered spell sent the letterman jacket's sleeve up to his elbow. The Wizard sliced the top of Brandt's forearm. Blood pooled into the narrow grooves in the metal.

"Fades!" Brandt yanked away. His old man beat him up, sure, but he'd never been cut open. He debated throwing an elbow at his attacker, dropping him to his knees and then knocking a fist into his temple.

"Relax. It's shallow, not to mention necessary."

Tristan found the place Brandt had smacked, and slammed the bloodied blade straight through, in line with the yellow dashes on the pavement. The barrier gave, sliced without a ripple. The tall man nodded with satisfaction, gripped a misty edge, and gestured to Brandt.

"After you."

18

NICU

*A*t nine years old, The Fae gave Nicu a mandate. Limit the Trimarked Child's movements within Trifecta.

Her presence was a daily reminder of magic. By remembering, the humans gained resistance to the Fae's dampening spells. Softening aggression was only possible if the humans themselves preferred to live in peace. Segregation equalled protection, and Ember was to be removed from school, and distanced from humans.

Though she was only seven, Nicu knew the girl's strength of will would make his task difficult. If he failed, Nicu would be disgraced. Cursed as he was with a Terran birth and the touch of the Trimark, his purpose would be extinguished. No master would apprentice him. No Fae would befriend him. He'd be little better than a prisoner within Center, and Branna would be trapped with him.

Nicu walked a careful line of understanding the need for control, yet not believing Ember was inherently dangerous because she was human and reckless. He thought he'd managed the best compromise by granting her a promise.

The Fae did not approve of his methods. He had been

forgiven because his method worked. His transgression had not been forgotten, though, as proof with Edan's presence.

So far, Edan had followed Nicu's lead with Ember. Would he continue to do so with new information? Nicu could not ignore the evidence. Brandt hurt the hybrid girl. A dramatic wave shook the barrier. Aaron was looking for Brandt. The direction was clear, and it was likely Brandt was outside Trifecta. Nicu categorized the event as nonthreatening to the Fae. Would Edan conclude the same?

Nicu scanned the main courtyard as he entered Center in search of Edan. Fae relaxed into their social hours under the purple sunset sky, dressed for comfort and warmth. They mingled between a ring of carts that had been wheeled between the transformed cabins. Potted fires were strategically placed to help keep the gathering warm as they collected their evening meal from one cart, a choice of drink from another.

Edan was not in attendance.

It was possible Edan had not witnessed Brandt's attack on Ember. There was little chance he hadn't discovered the truth of it. How deep into Trimark secrets had Edan delved? What did his second plan to do with that information? Had he already gone to the council? Nicu needed to find out.

Wist stopped Nicu's search with his heavy presence. Nicu cleared his mind, refused to assume the reason for the encounter.

"Come."

Nicu breathed into the moment, shifted his thoughts to more quiet avenues, eased the tension in his shoulders to allow the flexibility of multiple reactions.

The pair entered what had once been a rustic human place of worship and was currently the decorated council chamber. Dimmed light from polished, enchanted pillars stood guard at the edge of the room with tapestries hung between them, woven with sophisticated designs telling of the Fae's rich history. The council used the hall for Center business. For now, the building doors shut behind them, the long benches as empty as the board table on the raised dais.

Nicu would not speak first, especially here. Wist chose this space for what it represented, their differences in rank and power. He took a seat at the edge of a bench, motioned for Nicu to take the same position opposite the aisle. The Elder chose to sit below. Nicu could only sit where told.

"The barrier?" Wist asked.

Nicu allowed himself a breath.

"Complete."

"Hmm." The Elder arranged his long woven sweater, pulled it across his torso. "Humans?"

"The same."

Wist folded his hands together. "And the Trimarked Child?"

Was this where he learned Edan had chosen?

The power of a ten-year-old promise held Nicu's tongue still against the will of the Fae. Nicu's core tightened as the two points of control within his life battled. He reminded himself Ember had done nothing against the Fae. He would not extend that statement with the word, 'yet,' as Wist would.

"Is your mistake going to prove a problem?" Wist's warning pervaded as deep as obligation. "I did not think I needed to mention her specifically when we spoke earlier. Perhaps I should have."

"I follow the will of the Fae." Nicu's smooth answer betrayed none of the trepidation burning a hole in his chest.

"Indeed. Unfortunately, will is not always enough. For example, I meant to end the threat of the aberration. It was too late." Wist's mouth twisted on the taste of an awful memory.

Nicu marked each second of his inhale, counted out on his exhale.

"We cannot let chaos win," Wist said. "We cannot let the power of that star undo the work we've put into Trifecta. This is not perfect. It is not... home. But Gypsum is dying. We must continue to encourage the humans to accept us. Look at what challenges we can eliminate. I need you to do what needs to be done. Do what I could not."

Edan had not spoken to Wist. This was a different, more treacherous conversation. Should Nicu anticipate a direct order to modify his edict, a threat to the balance he'd so far maintained?

"Is this from the council, Elder?"

"We must contain the damage."

Had Wist found evidence of danger that Nicu had not?

Nicu blinked, careful to keep the motion natural. The potential change called unseen forces into the conversation. Time tested promises of the past against words of the future. Fate waited with bated breath to see if the scale would tip.

Magic grew thick in the air. Nicu held each heartbeat to a steady rhythm, forced every muscle to remain relaxed. The Elder watched for signs of Nicu's inner battle, to discover if promise or legacy would prove stronger.

All the Elder needed to do was share a new piece of knowledge and change Nicu's mandate. While Wist considered his options behind unchanging jet eyes, magic pooled and held Nicu prisoner to his choices.

Power broke.

The tension in the air burst out and away from Nicu's body. Burning pain thrust into the base of Nicu's skull. His back arched at the ambush, teeth clenched against the phantom attack.

Truth kept him from panic. No promise had broken, no action had him forsworn. This was not because of Wist.

The force plunged and carved through the nerves in his spine. He forced breath into his lungs at max capacity, and directed his concentration toward the purposeful discomfort in his chest rather than the actual attack. Attention diverted, he discovered reverberations of power from the strike, energy to track and follow.

Living Ink reacted. The waves marking his skin flowed from his limbs, swirled across his back, fast growing vines taking purchase against his vertebra.

"There's a barrier breach," he ground out as he focused on the cause of the pain. "Human land. End of the World."

The Elder towered over Nicu, face ashen. He disappeared from view, shouted for scouts the moment he threw open the door. Nicu held on to the power, looked for the source, for the reason. He searched for any hint of the Trimarked Child, a sign that this came from her.

Steel and blood coated the rupture.

Blood was a type of magic itself, an energy of life, ordered by control but with the potential to feed the chaos of the mind. A difficult power to tap into, harder to trace as it faded with healing, nearly impossible when done at such a range.

Nicu did it, anyway.

He held to the scent like a bloodhound, explored the speckled trail until he found the owner.

Not Ember.

Brandt Miller had returned to Trifecta with a magical artifact.

The pain needed to be stopped so Nicu could act.

Nicu closed his eyes. He gripped his fists in his lap and willed the edges of the tear together, fought to hold on over the distance. Severed lines of magic wove in and around each other to close the gap.

The agony against his back dissipated.

Nicu surged to his feet, ignored the flash of black vision, refused the wave of vertigo that jeopardized his stride until he hung against the door Wist had left open. Branna appeared, Edan not far behind, called by the commotion in the courtyard.

Nicu did not have time to ask old questions. He needed action.

"Find her."

This time, Edan went without argument, and with Branna as his shadow.

Nicu clenched his jaw and eased the door shut on the tumult outside, careful not to bring attention to the movement. He could not go, not so soon after Wist's test, an assessment that had proved just how delicate his position was. He'd fooled himself once again into thinking he'd found stable footing when all he had was practice and experience with the familiar.

Sworn to the Fae, bound by his promise, he found only a few, unexpected words could destroy him. He thought the hybrid girl would be the one to threaten his stability. Wist had illuminated his error.

Nicu refused to be forsworn, refused to lose his balance.

He needed options, knew where to find them.

The Fae would not approve.

Once he reached the dais at the back of the room, Nicu paralleled the rise toward the right. He moved a heavy tapestry, slipped behind, and made sure the hanging concealed him before he opened the hidden passageway.

A steep dirt ramp led into the dark, sandwiched between the council chamber and a storage closet. The hall was narrow to better disguise the added space. It widened under the building, allowing him to stop side-stepping and face forward once more.

No lights flickered, no enchanted wood set off a glow. Nicu counted off seconds, adjusted for pace, but still stumbled when the ramp stopped at the stone floor. One hand stretched before him, whispered numbers accompanied each cautious step into the black.

The labyrinth sat deep beneath the ground, another layer deeper than the underground halls that housed the Fae. Hard packed earth lined the surrounding walls. The artisans had placed the floor stones uneven and loose to make each movement forward a potential hazard. He closed useless eyes and remembered what he experienced during his single visit to the maze.

Some turns were dead ends, others confusing loops. There were few, however, that led to Fae relics and rare treasures brought through the Fade. Nicu was only familiar with one path. He had only been down here when the council showed him the source of his connection to the barrier. The artifact was not from old Gypsum, but of Center. They wanted him to realize the danger so he understood to ignore its draw.

He allowed the power to call to him now, used it to guide him as fingertips marked each turn taken and each path crossed. As a Fae, Nicu recognized the cost of chaos, the ability of High Magic to extract too great a fee. Yet, that same magic had saved and bound him. The chaos of life, rather than price. Perhaps it would help again.

Nicu's lungs labored in thin air. Sweat coated his brow with the effort it took to move forward, to fight the need for rest. The dark threatened to take him in too deep, to keep him trapped beneath the earth with no way out. The feelings were brought on by protective spells and he ignored them, except to note he must be close.

Then his fingers struck a small wooden box, pushed it away. It fell from its perch on a narrow pedestal. Nicu's hand shot out, gripped the solid wood before it plunged. There were no other protections here, the path itself able to deter any but the most determined.

He felt for the clasp, made sure the container faced top-side up before he opened the lid.

Nicu's fingers brushed cool metal. Delicate chains draped over his wrist. He traced the outline of a circle, followed the curved edges of a butterfly, found the intricate twists within the wing, the straight lines inside the circle as they crisscrossed into the shape of a star. This pentacle was not sealed with a slash. The Trimarked Child's Binding Ink was meant to block access. The talisman Nicu cupped in his palm ensured control of that power, not by Ember, but by whoever possessed the medallion.

Nicu dropped the box. It landed on the unseen floor with a muted crunch. His thumb rested on the pentacle. The star within the circle connected to the half butterfly, intended to restrict growth in an undesired direction. There was another form, as with all things.

Engaging the Trimarked Child's power was absolutely forbidden, even if used for the Fae. Yet, it might become paramount to ensure no other Fae had to sacrifice themselves for the hybrid girl's sake, that Nicu could handle any threat on his own. This pendant provided choice, and possibly a way to preserve balance should Wist press his cause.

The Fae would not approve.

He debated finding the box, replacing it and the talisman, walking away. That meant his options would be limited, if not now, then soon. Options he found himself compelled to keep.

Time ran out, choices came without warning, without opportunity to plan.

He needed choices, even those to be used as a last resort.

Nicu tied the medallion beneath heavy braids, the metal warmed where it pressed at the nape of his neck, at the very spot he'd experienced the first cut of a phantom blade and tried not to think how the very act felt like a decision had been made.

19

EMBER

*T*he thin foam mattress had never been so uncomfortable. Or was it her body? The bruise on her throat left her neck stiff. Every muscle wrung out and overused. Distant aches flared to life as she tossed and turned. Each bone ground against its neighbor when she lay still.

She would wake up her mother at this rate. The exterior of their house might be made of concrete blocks, but the interior was uninsulated, thin drywall.

Ember sat up and pulled on her layers, added a third layer of socks and two more hoodies to what she wore during the day. In a box at the head of her bed, she dug out a set of gloves and hat she turned inside out to hide the embroidered Trifecta High logo. Ember tried to pick the threads out once, but the knit had threatened to unravel, so she'd left it. At least it kept her warm.

She paused to enjoy the last few minutes of day fading on the horizon. She thought midnight would greet her instead of dusk. Apparently time crawled while your brain tangled itself up in no-win situations. The ice-tinted evening helped clear her thoughts a bit as her body struggled to keep warm and used up the energy needed for obsessing.

Ember watched deep purple fade to indigo. The horizon here fell downward, the sun taking its sweet time melting into the other side of the world. Morning brought a gentle warning before the sudden and bright arrival from behind mountain peaks. More days than not, she experienced both ends of the journey.

She'd never been so torn on what to do next, though. Bed proved a painful place and uncomfortable was the last thing Ember wanted to be. If Nicu turned her over to the Fae, she doubted they would keep her comfort in mind.

The underground club might be open, but as far as Ember knew it wasn't a twenty-four-hour hang out. Even the unwanted denizens had places to sleep for the night. She must remember Nicu's order, too, the only one she felt the need to follow.

That's not true.

It doesn't count when you're seven.

Well, fade it. Her brain decided it wasn't too frozen to think anymore. Ember refused to walk down memory lane, however, so that meant she should go someplace else. Her feet crunched through dying grass in the only direction that wouldn't lead her into someone else's territory - back into the forest.

She stumbled when dry, icy heat thrust between her eyes and stole her breath and vision. Ember staggered up the hill. Relief and horror blended when the torture released her mind, but split her face to her collar bone. Before she reached the tree line, her heart stopped, agony sliced through muscle. She dropped to all fours with a gasp and braced herself. The deep, precise pain tore down, dissected her sternum, carved through her stomach into her pelvis where it parted, moved to cramp every inch of tissue in her legs. Ember collapsed, flipped onto her back. She grabbed at her sweaters, pulled in search of what attacked.

A soft blue glow rose from the phantom cut and radiated

through her clothing. Ember raised her hands into the light, unsteady with its familiar touch. This matched barrier energy. But how?

Ember scrambled into a sitting position. The forceful torment turned into a grinding ache. She pushed herself back against the first of the trees.

Power brushed over Ember with sensations of pine and mist that reminded her of Nicu. She screamed as the invisible cut tugged closed, sharp pins along her ribs and thighs as if a million needles poked and prodded every portion of her pain. She searched the forest, desperate for sight of the Fae.

Was this Nicu? Did he make it impossible for her to disobey? Maybe she hadn't gotten off easy, after all?

The energy sewed together. The power flooded back in, now far too big. Ember grit her teeth against the pressure and tasted the salt of torrential tears. She turned into the forest and caught the safety of shadows. The crunch of leaves, the damp of dirt, did not register beyond the pain of being engorged.

Nicu promised.

}|{

The day had been horrible for Ember, one of the worst in her whole seven years. She kicked her grey tennis shoes, threw up the dead pine needles in her path, scowled at them as if they were the problem when the actual issue was left back at school.

Ember never made it to the swings first. That's all she wanted today, to be on a swing. She raced out to the playground right after lunch, not even eating all of it in her rush. It was worth it when she reached the swing, jumped on, got going.

Then someone shoved her off. She'd landed hard, the dirt pressed into the front of the yellow dress mom finished making for her a few days ago. The kid who stole her swing hopped on and took a running step back. Ember barely had time to roll out of the way before the bottom of their shoes shot toward her.

The grown ups pretended not to notice, not that part, anyway. Once they realized how dirty she was, they'd ordered her to the bathroom to clean up. Off the playground. Away from the other kids.

Ember hadn't gone back to class after that. She waited in a stall until recess finished, then escaped, and ran over the blacktop past the swings, through the grass field, on and on through Trifecta. She cut through yards and scrambled between bushes on her way home. Once there, she kept going into the forest, not wanting her mom to see the tears on her face.

"Stop."

Ember's feet stuck as if they were under an actual spell. Even as a nine-year-old Fae, Nicu was bossy. He didn't push her off swings, though.

"What do you want?" Ember asked.

"You're not permitted on Fae land." His hands rested on his hips, loose braids hung to his chin. He pointed above their heads. Ember looked up and huffed at the sight of heart-shaped leaves. Her eyes burned, her cheeks heated. Of course, she knew she wasn't allowed to go across that line. Her mom and Nicu had stressed the importance. A rule never to break.

She turned and walked away from the boundary and searched for a trail she recognized.

"It's that way." Nicu appeared at her side. She wanted to tell him she didn't need him to show her how to get home, but she did. She pursed her lips and let him take her. He didn't talk to her until they could see her house.

"You cannot go back to school."

Ember stumbled over a root and windmilled for balance. She skid a few feet down the hill, then turned to face him.

"Why?"

Nicu's steps were careful. He didn't slide. "You are a

reminder. As you grow, they look at you more, it affects them more. It will no longer be safe for you."

"But it's not fair. Why do they get more things than me? Why don't they just be nice?"

Nicu watched her tantrum with flat lips.

"Hybrid child," he snapped, then he took a deep breath. Ember counted to ten with him. She was still angry, but he had settled. "Listen. I will make you a promise, something Fae are not supposed to do because we have to keep them. Do you understand?"

Ember bit her lip and nodded.

"If you do this, if you stop going to school, don't try to be seen on purpose, I will make sure you're taken care of. I will make sure you're safe if you follow the rules."

Long before Ember understood what it meant, she agreed to a Fae's bargain.

)|(

Ember struggled through the forest, no longer certain why she moved or where she went. Her body bathed in misery, the echos of memory sent shock waves through her brain.

Nicu promised, she agreed. Then she forgot.

Be invisible.

Follow the rules.

"*You let him notice you.*" Words Nicu said recently, a warning.

Another pull across littered ground. Her hand flung out and dropped. Fell without pain.

Ember blinked. A clearing spread before her, a place where Nature had drawn a line in the forest to declare nothing should grow past this point.

No Man's Land. She knew of it. Her mother brought her once, but she never revisited since it was adjacent to both Fae and Witch borders.

Across that line, her hand did not hurt. The rest of her did. With a broken cry, Ember dug in, crawled forward with lunging motions, fell flat to her back and shuddered.

The power popped, then calmed, settled like a weight of water against her spine, trickled into the ground and beyond, deep underneath her, drawn from her body. The slashing and pinning she'd suffered through soothed away as if by a cool breeze, though no wind existed here.

Peace.

Ember closed her eyes and breathed.

20

AARON

*A*aron dropped into bed and threw his arm over his face. It had been an endless day since Brandt disappeared. After leaving Ember, Aaron headed out to check at his friends' house again and a few places he liked to go to blow off steam. Nobody had seen him, so at least Aaron hadn't wasted his time acting on his suspicion of Nicu.

Ember said he'd fallen off the edge. It was only a figure of speech. No one could leave Trifecta, but it appeared as if Brandt had done exactly that. Where was the jerk?

Did Aaron want to find him?

Aaron flipped to his side and threw a few punches into his pillow. His friend had become rough around the edges, and alcohol did not help the situation. The possibility that Brandt would attack Ember never crossed Aaron's mind, yet he had.

As long as it's only the Trimarked girl. He winced at Ember's remembered words, drew his hand over his face.

Verge, he didn't want who she was to be the reason it was okay. He hated that his first emotional reaction was understanding why Brandt thought attacking Ember was fine, when it wouldn't be with a human girl.

She shouldn't have forgiven him. He shouldn't have even asked for it. He was as much an asshole as Brandt.

Aaron flopped to his back, lifted and dropped his head a few times, stared at the ceiling.

Well, fades.

He sat up, searched the floor for his jeans and pulled them on. He gripped his rumpled t-shirt next, then tugged a thick puff-coat from his closet. His window slid open without a sound, and he swung both legs out. The bottom half of the house was bricked, the second story wrapped in siding. The brick gave Aaron's toes purchase while he drew the pane closed. He wouldn't come back this way, and it would throw his old man off if, against the odds, he checked in.

Aaron dropped to the ground, careful to bend his knees with the impact. Dad would flay him if he injured his knee during the season. He took quick stock, satisfied he hadn't strained anything, and put his coat on.

Street lights to his left, night to his right, Aaron kept in the middle and jogged through backyards. The ghostly shape of Ember's pale grey house rose from moon-silvered grass.

Someone was in her yard. Aaron slowed, squinted as if narrowed vision was what he needed to see in the dark. He approached the figure with quiet steps. Was it a Fae guard? Had Nicu returned with whatever consequences he'd threatened?

The guy shifted his profile, gripped something at his side, then raised his arm to stare at the knife in his hand.

"Verge." Aaron winced at the sound of his own voice and drifted to a stop when the boy turned to him. "Brandt."

Aaron's eyes swapped between his friend's face and the blade. Tension coiled through his shoulders. "What the hell are you doing? Where have you been?"

"Aaron? What are you doing here? Never mind. Wanna help me find the Trimarked girl?" Brandt's grip softened, but he didn't let go of the weapon or put it away.

"Why do you want to find her?" Aaron asked. Brandt's lips curled.

"Because the bitch threw me out."

"Of the party?"

"Of fading Trifecta!"

Aaron wanted to remind his friend that wasn't possible. Maybe Brandt had been so drunk last night he'd passed out and slept in the forest all day, hallucinating.

Except Ember's power had pushed Aaron away earlier.

"You choked her."

"And that's a good reason to push me out the barrier? Get me kidnapped by freaking wanna-be survivalists?"

Aaron swallowed his nausea, acutely aware he didn't have an answer. Was one worse? Was Brandt's anger justifiable?

"What are you going to do?"

"I have to find her," Brandt answered.

"You've knocked on her door?"

"No. She's not here," he spat, lifted the knife again. "This connects to her somehow. It kinda vibrates when it's close to her."

"Where did you get that?" Aaron's head felt light, his conscience torn.

"From the guy who got me back in."

Aaron understood why Brandt was pissed. He hoped the weapon was just to find Ember, but Aaron couldn't predict how far his friend might go. He remembered the speckled purple and red band across Ember's neck, wide enough to see how flattened she'd been.

"Come on, man. Let's get some sleep. You can stay over and we'll come back in the morning when she's home."

"Fuck that," Brandt countered. "It's part of the deal of getting back in. I've got to find her for that guy."

"Just find her?"

Brandt's smile rose along with an unapologetic shrug. "That's what he wants, but I get to talk to her first."

Aaron shoved his hands in his pockets, pushed down so the hood stretched.

"Okay. I'll come with you," he offered. "See what's going on."

"Cool." Brandt gestured toward the trees. "This thing says that way. With both of us, she won't be so quick to lock us out."

Brandt pulled out a pocket sized flashlight and turned on its bright, narrow beam. Aaron kept close, his attention torn between the shadows on Brandt's face and the bits of forest revealed in the light.

"You okay?" Aaron watched Brandt's reaction, tried to judge his friend's state of mind via his question.

"Yeah," Brandt answered with an easing in his tone as if all he'd waited for was for Aaron to check on him. Guilt weighed heavily in Aaron's chest, not sure why he hadn't asked before this. "I'm hungry and need a drink, but I'm a big boy. I can go longer."

"Nothing to drink?" Aaron double checked. Brandt's laugh indicated he took Aaron's words as a joke.

"I know, right? We'll grab one together after this. Celebrate."

"Yeah. Great. What are we celebrating?"

Brandt's grin twisted and grew in the odd combination of light and shadow. "Freedom."

Aaron debated asking for clarification but wasn't positive he wanted to hear the answer, not when he didn't know what Brandt planned to do with the knife. He held the thing at his side, raised it every now and again to scan the air, shifted direction due to vibrations Aaron couldn't detect. After about ten minutes, Brandt stopped and slipped the blade between the waistband of his jeans and leather belt.

"Here somewhere." Brandt illuminated the trees.

"In the middle of the forest?"

Brandt slowed the pass of light, this time lower toward the

floor of a natural clearing where three or four downed trunks had created space. Something on the ground caught Aaron's attention, and he waited for Brandt to bring the beam back over it.

"Em!" He recognized her supine form and scrambled forward, dropped next to her. Brandt kept the light on her while Aaron's shaking hands tapped her cheeks, touched her neck as if he knew how to check for a pulse. "Em, wake up."

Had Nicu come for her?

Brandt stepped to the other side of Ember's body. "She'd better be alive."

Aaron nodded, distracted as he checked for a heartbeat again, mindful of her bruise. Yes, there he felt her pulse.

"Y-yeah. Just out cold." Aaron tapped her shoulder, trying not to make her worse.

"Wake her."

"I'm trying!"

Brandt crouched, looked between the girl and Aaron, then shrugged. "If she's breathing, she'll come around soon enough. This is good. It will be easier to tie her up."

Aaron wrenched his attention onto Brandt. "What? Are you insane?"

Brandt lifted the pure-white beam level with Aaron's eyes.

"Me?" Brandt demanded. "She threw me out of Trifecta, Aaron. She has control over the barrier and keeps us trapped. I'm not the one who's crazy. I'm not the one fawning all over her like a love-sick puppy."

"What are you talking about?"

"What was that you called her? Em? Are you friends with the mutt, Aaron? Is that why you got me off her yesterday?"

Aaron's heartbeat sped up three-fold at the venom in his friend's tone. He tried to look beyond the blinding flashlight, but Brandt kept it on him.

"That was about Nicu."

"As if the two of us couldn't take on a single Fae." Aaron's shoulders twitched, remembered the controlled strength in Nicu's one arm, fingers curled up around his neck, body pinned, his struggle forward all but ignored.

"You got it wrong."

"Gonna deny it?" Brandt unzipped his coat and dropped a length of rope onto Ember's chest. "Then get to it."

Brandt lowered the flashlight to the rope. Aaron blinked away blind spots, froze when he saw his friend had retrieved the knife and stood over him.

"What the hell? Are you going to stab me if I don't? We've been friends since fourth grade."

"Exactly. You and me. Not that bitch. So prove it."

That's when Aaron realized he'd been waiting for Nicu to make one of his magical appearances, to take over and decide what to do with Brandt so he wouldn't have to. His stomach sunk. He looked at Ember and wondered if her punishment was why Nicu wasn't here.

Brandt's grip shifted on the knife. He knew how to hold it, how to use it. Where had he learned that?

Aaron reached toward Ember. He jolted her shoulder. Her body's reaction was passive. She would not wake up.

He grabbed the rough fibers of the rope and imagined tying it around Ember's wrists, how it would rub against her skin like sandpaper. The point of the blade rose a fraction.

"Why do you need her tied up to talk to her?"

"Verge." Brandt stared at Aaron, his breathing loud, his voice scratchy. "I get it now. First she kicks me out, then she goes after my best friend."

"That is not what happened. I went after her to find you."

"Yeah. Yeah, that makes even more sense. Then she hexed you."

Aaron stiffened at the sharp turn of Brandt's logic.

"What are you talking about?"

"Dude. It's okay. I'll fix it." Brandt stepped over Ember's legs and Aaron stood up to face him.

"What—"

Brandt stabbed the knife deep into the top of Aaron's thigh. Aaron cried out in pain and shock, his hands pressed against fresh blood.

"Sorry, man, I'm so sorry, but I don't know how strong her spell is and I can't have you helping me, not messed up like you are."

Aaron could only gape as the weight of Brandt's fist drove into his jaw.

21

EMBER

*E*mber woke up to a dull ache, grateful the sharp edges and constant pressure had eased. She shifted on the hard ground. Her choice of bedding did not help her feel less sore. How long had she been asleep? And out in the forest?

She tried to sit up, but her arms stuck. They contorted behind her back, awkward and useless. She twisted her wrists, froze when rope rasped against skin.

Her hands were tied. Okay.

Ember stilled her movement and listened to the world around her. Calling out wouldn't benefit her if no one was there to help. She also didn't want her attacker to know she was awake until... what? She got more information? The best plan was to let them believe she was knocked out until the moment they were ready to untie her.

"Ahh, shit, Aaron." Wait. Was that Brandt? "Blood is soaking your pants."

"That's what happens when you get stabbed." Aaron's voice strained with pained fatigue.

"Yeah. Sorry I hit you, too. I thought... well, I'm glad you're okay. You took that punch like it was just another bounce against the barrier."

"I've had a boxing lesson recently," Aaron said.

What in the realms had happened while she'd been passed out? Ember gave in and opened her eyes. It was difficult to see, but she guessed she lay on the edge of No Man's Land. Aaron leaned against a fallen trunk, one knee bent, the other stretched out. Brandt stood off center, closer to her than his friend and back-lit by the flashlight he held. He turned the beam onto Aaron's legs, and Ember's breath caught. That looked like a lot of blood.

"Here." Brandt searched his pockets. "This was to gag her, but you need it more." He pulled out a strip of cloth and strode to Aaron's side. "Do you want—"

"I got it." Aaron snatched the bandana and tied it at the top of his thigh with a grunt. "So I can leave? You don't mind?"

"Yeah, go. Take care of yourself. We can catch up later."

"You're just going to wait for your friend?"

"Aaron, man, get out of here before you bleed to death."

Aaron scrambled to his feet. His eyes flickered toward Ember, but returned to Brandt. He tested his weight on his leg, hissed through gritted teeth, then set off.

He left her there, tied up with Brandt, the guy who was pissed with her.

Ember hoped Aaron got hopelessly lost in the dark.

Unless he found help. Then let him go straight and true.

The flashlight dazzled her vision, a reminder she should pretend to sleep. Too late now. Brandt towered over her and kept her blinded.

"See him leave you? Yeah, that's because of me. His actual friend." Ember remained silent, mostly because he was only making half sense. The part she understood snuffed her little spark of hope.

Ember reinforced her wish that Aaron lose his way.

"You think a day of chasing your tail matters? He was only looking for me. He found me, too." A chest thump echoed the pride Brandt laced into his words. "I'm not sure what you thought to get out of him. Street cred? A kid with more human blood than mutt? You're not even his type."

Ember's brow furrowed. "Brandt, are you okay?"

"Okay? Okay! That's rich coming from the person who caused all this."

"Are you hurt?" She asked because he clearly looked for some reaction, some connection, or he wouldn't ramble so much. If she calmed him, pretend to care, he might untie her. He had, at the very least, stopped light blinding her. "We can find help—"

"Nobody hurt me. I got away." His glare burned with hate. "You won't."

Brandt ran a hand over his face, lengthened each of his features. He dropped to the ground beside her, propped himself against the tree. Ember twisted her torso to put a few more inches between them. Brandt's hands trembled and his flashlight danced, illuminated the dark circles under his eyes.

"I'm so tired. But that's okay. After this I can go home and sleep in a fading bed again."

Brandt leaned his head back and fell asleep.

Ember squinted, did not trust his deep breathing or the sudden slack in every muscle of his body. No one passed out that fast. Did they?

She watched for a few more minutes, then struggled into a sitting position, winced at the strain and wished she'd taken Chase up on more boxing lessons. Brandt didn't stir despite her movement or the corresponding noise.

Ember almost pitched forward while standing up, but stumbled into a tree. Her shoulder jammed against the unforgiving trunk and kept her upright. She found her balance, cheek pressed into the valleys and peaks of the thick, rough bark, and stood.

There wasn't enough light to check for directions. She assumed Aaron headed toward Town. Fae land was forbidden to her. She turned her back against the direction she thought led to Center, irritated at her obedience, compelled by a need to follow the rules after so many disasters.

She wouldn't take Aaron's path. Ember couldn't be certain of his motivations and didn't know if he was reliable. Other humans wouldn't save her, and Susan wasn't able to in her delicate state. That left the Witches, a group she had a decent shot with, especially if Devi had ended up in Ember's debt.

A soft snore vibrated through Brandt. Her cue to get moving and fast, not sure if the noise of her departure would penetrate his nap. Ember twisted her arms while she walked and tested the rope. All she earned were sore wrists. She needed to be free, craved speed so she could put yards instead of feet between her and Brandt. How far away was the Circle? She might run into one of their patrols. She could do this.

A hand clutched the length of her trailing hair and yanked.

Ember's shriek dissolved into a deep sob. Of course, he caught her. He ran every fading day of his life.

The knife was unexpected. He pressed the blade against her ribs. Fingers twisted in her hair and secured her against him, his mouth hot and sickly humid against her ear.

"Sorry, but you're going in the wrong direction. Besides, we can't go anywhere without this knife or the Witches will find us.

"S-so, it's just to hide us?" She choked on the words. Her lungs ached from her rush through the forest. Brandt lifted the blade inches from her face.

"It cuts real nice, too," he promised. Ember closed her eyes, swallowed her cry. Aaron's leg.

Ember hooked her foot behind Brandt's, then slammed them both backward. He grunted, took the brunt of their fall, stunned enough to let go of her hair. She rolled away from his knife hand until her legs were up and ready to kick and defend. Brandt scrambled on all fours, and shoved her calves to the side. His knee landed on her stomach, his fist gripped her shoulder, the blade against her neck.

"This will be easier if you aren't bleeding or knocked out, but I can carry your wounded ass through this forest if you make me."

He added pressure to the knife. The flow of power inside her twisted. Internal energy she associated with the border retracted from the weapon like prey recognizing a predator. But it had come to her defense and stiffened between her and Aaron.

Something was not right, something more than a pissed off bouncer.

"Who let you back in?"

"Someone a hell of a lot nicer than you," Brandt said. "He even helped me so the kumbaya spell the Fae set doesn't blur my mind again."

"Kumbaya?" Ember felt lost, not sure she followed him.

"Yeah. You know about that, too? So we don't fight too hard at having mages take over more than half our land?"

Ember shook her head, more to relieve a headache than in answer. Brandt took it as one, anyway.

"Well, maybe they cast that on you, too. Or maybe you don't need it. Doesn't matter. The point is, my friend wants to meet you, but first, you and I have some unfinished business."

Ember's stomach sunk. Unfinished business was never pleasant. If she stayed alert, she might escape Brandt again and hide this time instead of run, preferably before they met up with his mysterious benefactor. Instinct flared and cautioned that whoever this secret, obviously magical stranger was, they were the exact opposite of nice.

Ember stumbled when Brandt shoved her forward. He held her hair like a leash. The hand with the knife rested against her ribs as Brandt kept their bodies close.

I take it back. Let Aaron's path be the right one. Let his leg hold strong. Somehow, let him find Chase.

Please.

22

AARON

*A*aron liked to win. He liked to train to overcome. Pain was a sign of power for him, that he pushed his body further, faster, harder even when it fought back. His teammates hated his drive during practice, depended on it during games. It's how he earned the title of captain.

He imagined his awkward stride and the weakness in his thigh was from one too many leg presses in the gym. His lack of energy from a ten-mile run. The stress on his body meant nothing against the promise of success.

This would be his most important win. He refused to lose.

Aaron burst past the tree line. He'd misjudged, came out closer to his back yard than Ember's. He adjusted, grit his teeth and forced his vision to tunnel toward the goal ahead.

The door to the underground stuck. Aaron's heart stuttered, afraid it was locked until it wrenched open on a desperate pull. Aaron shouted into the passageway, not knowing if anyone heard him past the steel portal at the other end of the hall. The wall held him up when his wounded leg dragged, his vision pin-holed against the struggle.

No, not done yet.

"Chase!" He called, air forced so firmly that his lungs flattened and he coughed in response to the negative pressure. "Chase!"

His knee buckled, fingernails bent back as he scrambled for purchase on the wall.

"Whoa, there." A beefy set of hands caught under Aaron's arms, slowed his fall from a crash to a sit. Aaron blinked away the blur, made out Keegan's wide features.

"Chase," Aaron rasped.

"Wrong guy. Keegan, remember?" Aaron nodded, his grip clutched Keegan's forearm with the force of urgency.

"Ember."

This time Keegan understood. He turned and opened the door, only three feet away from where Aaron had fallen.

He'd almost made it. He'd made it far enough.

"Chase isn't here, yet." Keegan's tone flattened along with the line of his lips. He chose one of the couches in the middle to drop Aaron onto, then ran to the kitchen for towels.

Aaron looked around to see not only was Chase gone, but so was everyone else, other than Keegan. The movement sent blackout pain behind his eyes. He groaned, his hand clenched against his hip and he tilted his head back, breathed deeply to fight the nausea.

Chase appeared from one of the doorways.

"Keegan, I need—"

"Aaron's hurt," Keegan interrupted, running back to the couch with the towels. "Ember's in trouble."

Chase wasted no time. He knelt on the floor at Aaron's side, moved the human's hand out of the way and pulled the jean fabric apart to check out the wound.

Aaron was strong. He did not swoon. Except for when he lost about a gallon of blood and most of the feeling in his leg until it screamed to life when someone pressed on it. Then he might swoon.

Chase leaned in, watched Aaron's eyes focus and clear.

"Is Ember hurt?"

"Not when I left."

"Could she be?" Aaron frowned, thought about what Brandt had said.

"Not yet. She's with—"

Chase pulled back and asked Keegan for water and hard liquor, cutting off Aaron's attempt to explain. The words flew further from his mind when he felt wiry fingers at his belt buckle. He struggled to sit, pressed up with his good leg, and watched Chase working to get his pants off.

"What—"

"Can you push up?" Chase asked. "Once I untie this hand-kerchief, the blood will gush. You've lost a ton already. Can you do it or does Keegan?"

"But Ember—"

"You, or Keegan, or your leg." The words stopped Aaron's protest and his choice.

Aaron did not like to lose, especially when they were talking about his limb.

"Yeah. I got it."

"Go." Chase untied the cloth in one pull. Aaron thrust his hips and cried out as his jeans tore from skin, glued by his blood. Chase left the waistband at Aaron's knees before the Halfer's palm pressed into the wound.

"Whiskey," Chase demanded. "And get him something to bite."

The alcohol burned down to Aaron's bones where Chase poured it over the deep cut. Keegan threw a wooden spoon into his mouth just before his teeth clashed with enough force to crack the handle. Aaron held on to it against nausea and faint, watched the pale gold liquid mix with coppery blood and spill onto the couch in a muddy mess.

Chase tugged a velvet pouch from around his neck. He dumped out a handful of different stones, searched for some-thing purple and another that looked like a lump of frosted glass. The hand with the gems slapped on top of the one staunching Aaron's wound, and Chase chanted.

The healing was raw and forceful. Chase's voice grew louder against Aaron's guttural cry. Keegan sat on Aaron's calves. One arm reached around Chase to push Aaron's torso down when he tried to sit up.

Chase fell back to the floor, the two gems lost somewhere beside him.

"Sorry that sucked. I'm not a full Wizard, clearly, but I wanted to make sure the muscle healed right. I know how you jocks get when you can't play anymore."

Keegan lifted his weight from Aaron's body. After handing Aaron a cup of water with a trembling hand, Chase toasted the air with his own glass, and downed the liquid in thick, long gulps. Exhausted, still in shock, Aaron found himself mesmerized by the bob of Chase's Adam's apple, then coughed and focused on his own water, though he didn't want it.

"Drink," Keegan ordered. "Just like after a game."

Aaron jerked a nod, took a small sip before thirst caught up and he tipped it back in a direct copy of Chase.

The fog cleared as Aaron drank and his body reacted to the promise of replenished liquid. He realized he was half naked. Using the clean part of a towel to dry off as quickly as he could, Aaron shimmied back into the ruined fabric of his jeans. Decent once again, he offered his cup to Keegan who refilled it from a banged up pitcher.

"I'd appreciate you not saying anything about my Working magic," Chase asked. "Only Keegs here knows of all the Halfers."

Aaron nodded, his eyes closed as he breathed through the adrenaline crash.

"You said something about Ember."

Chase's reminder slapped Aaron in the face. How could he forget? Asshole status retained, Aaron wiped drips of water from his chin with a curse, pressed against the back of the couch to get up. Keegan's free hand landed on his head and pushed him back.

"Don't make me tell Keegan to sit on you again," Chase suggested with a wry twist to his mouth. "Just talk."

"Brandt has her. He got back in somehow."

"Where is she?" Chase asked.

"In the forest."

"That is the least helpful bit of information."

"No," Aaron challenged. "I know how to get there. I've been there and back. Besides, it's... weird. Nothing grows there. I swear the wind even stopped —"

Chase surged to his feet, yanked his zipper to his chin. "No Man's," he announced. Aaron swatted Keegan's hand away and stood up before they restrained him again.

"No," Chase ordered.

Aaron scowled. He'd given the guy his due earlier while here with Ember. That did not give him the right to order Aaron around like he was one of his other lackeys.

"I'm going."

"You'll fall behind."

Aaron snorted, arms crossed over his chest. The skin on his torso had started to warm and it felt oddly shaped, like the Witch's drawing. Probably his body trying to recover. He ignored it like the order to stay behind. He stared Chase down, dared him to think any of his guys could outrun him, out-stamina him, hurt or not. Aaron did not lose.

Chase softened his approach, but not his resolve. "I fixed a cut, stitched your muscle, but replacing lost blood is beyond me."

"I'll lose something more if I don't go."

"Ember," Chase guessed. Aaron jerked a nod. "You've known her for a day."

"I fading left her with a psycho," he ground out. "I can't leave it at that."

"I'll take it from here. It's why you came to me. So sit the verge down."

"No."

Chase stepped up, chest to chest. "You know you had me fooled. I thought you stumbled in here because you wanted to live."

"I want to save Ember."

"Big words. Why this sudden connection to someone you've happily ignored until now?"

"She forgave me."

Chase's eyes narrowed. Anger flushed his cheeks and pulled his shoulders back. With a curse, he twisted away from Aaron.

"How in the realms did you manage that?"

Aaron shrugged. "I asked her to."

Chase gaped at the human. His dry, harsh laugh echoed in the empty room. "Right. You asked her and just like that, the Trimarked gave you a pardon." Chase studied Aaron from an angle. A grudging smile lined his mouth.

"You get your way, Harwell. But you better keep up because I'm not waiting."

"No sweat," Aaron drawled, certain he wouldn't be the one trailing. "Do you need your stones?"

Chase shook his head.

"That shit takes too long."

A grin ticked Aaron's lips and he jogged to catch up, eager to show Chase he wasn't going to back down until the last whistle blew.

23

TRISTAN

*T*he forest offered so many superb shadows to hide in, more than Tristan remembered, though having no reason to leave them proved unexpected. The chosen location of No Man's Land was empty for now, the quarry gone astray and uninvited guests about to crash the cancelled party. What a mess.

Save him from the impatient.

It was not Tristan's preference to leave things to chance, such as what happened with this young human, turned negligent accomplice. Attaining the aid of one of the outsiders would have been preferable. At least they were disciplined and mission focused. Though, as no one got in or out without the Trimarked Child, their stated purpose felt questionable.

They were also very loyal. That appeared to be a qualifying factor for their positions. No weak links there.

Until the last one. They had not welcomed Brandt's unplanned appearance and did not mind his escape. After that, the easy-to-manipulate boy provided the needed entry fee. All Brandt had to do in return was set up a fortuitous meeting and perform introductions. This would provide the chance to establish expectations between those in attendance.

Brandt's sour attitude had helped at the onset, but thoughts of revenge were getting in the way. Now the teenager followed his own small-minded idea instead of the important one.

An authentic example of youth being wasted on the young. Luckily, Tristan could make adjustments. He would set aside the original plan. At least the timeline remained intact.

For now, the focus continued to be alienating the Child, taking away support systems. She seemed to have one main crutch that, if taken out, would serve double duty of leaving her unbalanced and with a loss of purpose.

In other words, vulnerable. Vulnerable meaning malleable. Malleable meaning willing. Willing being the most important synonym of all.

Time to visit an old friend.

24

NICU

*N*icu climbed from the labyrinth and found the faint outline of the council chamber's door. He left the tunnels and paused behind the curtain to let his eyes adjust while he patted dust motes and cobwebs from his clothing. Even though the room sounded empty, Nicu practiced caution, peeking from between the heavy tapestry and the wood column before he emerged from hiding.

He jogged through the building, exited and closed up the chamber, another layer to hide where he'd been.

The seven members of the Elder Council stood near the entrance, dressed in wraps decorated with their ancestral patterns. If they had drawn their meeting inside, he would be trapped behind the tapestry. The mass of Fae before them saved him from immobility or discovery, their numbers too great to fit within the chamber.

Nicu used the confusion to mask his insertion into the swarm, listening to the surrounding snippets to catch up.

"The scouts found the point of entry…"

"… how do Fae scouts lose the trail ten feet in?"

"Nicu!" Wist called. The crowd didn't part, but eased around him as he answered the summons.

"Elder Councilors," he greeted with a bow.

"Have you recovered?" Elder Ethna questioned, her hair braided up her scalp, the length spun into a balanced twist atop her head.

"Yes, Elder."

"Was it a grave hurt, having taken an hour to mend?" Wist asked. Confirmation his absence had been noticed.

"No, Elder. I repaired the damage."

"Without council permission?" Elder Neyu's wrap rustled with his agitation.

"My apologies. It was manipulation, not casting, returning energy to its preferred state." He neglected to include his pain would have continued without the repair, lest the council consider the choice selfish, as opposed to protective.

"That being the case," Wist admonished. "We could have evaluated the tear for usefulness. An exit into the larger world may have proven beneficial. We assume our peace with the humans only works because there are so few of them in Trifecta. Perhaps an excursion out would allow us to test that theory."

"At least this way we will know if the interloper tries to escape," Elder Ethna said. "We can study the rupture, find the mechanism that caused it and see if Nicu's fix is reversible."

"We should also learn from this and discuss increasing patrols on the human side. We could claim they're hunting parties," Elder Neyu insisted. "I will work on different options to review."

"Agreed," Wist said. "Nicu, study the tear as Elder Ethna suggested. We shall meet in the morning and receive your report."

Dismissed, Nicu bent lower before he straightened for departure. He overlooked the way the crowd parted for him this time through, their eyes bright with awareness, their ability to ignore him suspended with evidence of his purpose having import.

Wary approval filled the air, cautious acceptance. Nicu disregarded it all. Attention and fame had never been his aim. His duty was important, not his person, and he left to perform it while they continued socializing.

Once in the forest a presence he had not expected derailed him from pursuing the barrier investigation. Feet slowed, he rounded a tree to discover Branna and Edan shared a perch, their closest hands loose at their sides, pinkies brushed as if by accident. As soon as the pair noticed Nicu, their limbs drew inches apart. Their contact was not what bothered him, however.

"You were to find her."

"We cannot," Edan said.

Nicu inhaled around the frustration, expelled it on his breath.

"Explain."

"The obvious?" Branna asked. "She is not at home, or underground, or off with Chase."

She'd gone to ground. To escape after this afternoon?

No.

Why hadn't he thought Ember might have felt the barrier breach as he had? He had not found her signature and had forgotten they were both tied to the same energy.

"She's hurt."

Nicu launched into a sprint. Edan and Branna followed without question, highlighting their value. He could not waste time on explanation. More than an hour had passed since he discovered the taint of Brandt's blood mixed with the magic of a knife used to carve someone's way into Trifecta.

That meant two enemies, one unknown who could breach the barrier, and one with a personal grudge against the Trimarked Child, the hybrid girl who was suddenly lost.

Nicu arrived at the hovel the Lees called home and approached the entrance to the underground to examine the space where Ember had sparked. He searched the long, dead strands of mountain grass for a hidden trace of that power. Warm fragments brushed and stuck to fingertips, and he curled his fingers to protect his prize.

"You aren't welcome here."

Nicu stood to meet Susan's emaciated form, her thin shoulders wrapped in a threadbare afghan, storm grey eyes sharp with instant hostility.

"Susan Lee," he greeted, his voice low and soft.

"Why are you here? You need to leave. Now."

"Soon," he assured her. "Can you tell me, when was Ember home last?"

"Stay away from my baby!" She took a threatening step forward, a starved and cornered animal fighting for her life.

"Susan, she is lost," Nicu tried to reason. "When did you see her? Was she in any pain that you noticed?"

A flush bruised Susan's sharp cheekbones.

"I will never help a Fae. My daughter will not get involved with magic. I do not allow it in my house. You are not allowed."

"If you care for Ember, you will tell me."

The heat from Susan's cheeks rose to cast a glassy sheen over her eyes. Her breath came in hard pants.

"I won't let you murder my daughter. I would kill her first."

"Ember will not die." The words were a low command. A threat.

"I hope you don't find her," Susan spat at his feet. "I hope she gets free of you, no matter how."

Susan spun on her heel and stumbled as if drunk, though alcohol was not her affliction, and headed back into the safety of her house.

"She is insane," Branna whispered.

"She is sick, though currently not our concern." He looked at the energy he'd collected, the smallest whiff of power. Nicu encouraged his tattoos to move from his forearm and across his palm to engage with the salvaged fragments. The power of the

Living Ink tasted the flavor of Ember. He flicked his wrist, straightened his fingers and sparks flashed into the night, danced on an invisible breeze.

Lead the way. He willed the magic to find the being who created it.

Nicu refused to take his eyes off the glowing cloud. It hovered close to the ground, touched deep toward the forest floor, surged up as if infused with a sudden rush of temporary energy, only to drift low once again.

"She crawled," Edan said. Nicu's curse stayed within his mind. The flattened trail led through the foliage. Yet, he'd ignored it with his choice to focus so intently on their magic guide. Attention expanded, he regarded every lurch forward from that moment on, each trampled piece of leaf where she'd collapsed here, and then there.

"She was not injured badly," Branna said. "There is no blood."

"It was not a physical wound." Nicu imagined Ember's smaller, more fragile frame taking the pain he'd grit his teeth against. Remorse twisted through his organs and fear grew metallic in the back of his throat.

He refused to be forsworn, the cost far too high to pay.

He put aside those thoughts as unnecessary distractions to his current goal. Find Ember. Worry about the rest if it proved pertinent.

"Are you well?" Edan asked quietly.

Nicu remained silent, uncertain how to reply. Though they disagreed on how to handle the Trimarked Child, there was one truth they worked together to protect. His promise to keep her safe.

Discomfort rose anew when Nicu recognized a thick vine strangling a fading birch. A few feet further, a gentle mound marked the grave of a tree fallen one hundred years ago. The tender footsteps of his companions betrayed they were aware of the location.

Ember's chunky trail led to No Man's Land. Ember was not there.

The flecks flared bright the moment they touched No Man's Land, sped in all directions within the dead patch of forest, flew up toward the canopy and concentrated at the center, then dropped in a brilliant streak deep into the ground.

They did not reappear.

Edan and Branna stepped next to him, one on either side.

"There are tracks," Edan offered. "Multiple sets. We can split up, each take a path and report back once we find her."

Edan knew more than any other they must find Ember. The Terraborn, true bloodline Fae had been appointed to remind Nicu there should be no unapproved secrets from the Fae. Yet, Edan had not gone to the council with news of Ember's skill with the barrier, and he declared his loyalty by remaining steadfast this evening. Nicu would not offend by acting without thought.

He debated their options, knew this decision held either the weight of praise or the unbearable burden of broken magic.

"Someone comes." Branna turned her back to the dead zone, wrapped shadows around herself until she disappeared. Edan placed his body between Nicu and the coming threat, a gift of added time.

More than one set of footsteps stomped through the forest. To even the odds, Nicu spun and faced the incomers at Edan's side.

Nicu embodied control. When he saw a familiar figure limp through the trees, he merely stepped forward once, used the human's momentum to swing him around, his back to Nicu's chest, wrapped a forearm writhing with contained fury against the shout in that boy's throat, then held still without breaking every bone in Aaron's neck.

25

DEVI

*D*evi stood at the center of a complicated web, stretched nodal patterns and a multitude of connections. She spun in a slow circle within the golden globular network, a gentle smile on her face as she enjoyed the artistry of the magic.

"Your pupil nearly takes over your entire eye when you Work."

Leona's voice broke through Devi's concentration. She held out a hand. The bubble of power collapsed onto itself, brightened in her palm, then faded as the tubular shape of the gem reconfigured.

Leona gasped, her fingers spread and fluttered for a moment as she stared at the result. Her mother had never been comfortable with Devi's unique ability with magic, though as High Priestess, Leona saw the benefit of it. As a parent, however, Leona feared the differences in her daughter, not because she didn't accept them, but because she didn't know what they would mean for Devi. Usually, Leona ignored Devi's Work for those reasons. When presented with it, she wavered between her emotions until she settled onto a tentative perch of brave, but unwelcome acceptance.

"No scrying stone needed, after all."

"I got creative," Devi agreed.

"Are you closer to figuring out your puzzle?"

Devi crossed her legs, then spun to face the barrels. She had tested her crystal stretching with the gems that stored the oil composition.

"I figured out how to clean it, but the compounds produced would be difficult to manage. I will move on from trying to reclaim the waste to reconstructing the components into a usable material."

"So you're practicing with a quartz?"

"That was play. I wanted to make it bigger without losing its molecular structure."

"O-oh." Leona fidgeted with her bracelets, then stilled her fingers by gripping her wrist.

Truthfully, the exercise had been exciting. Though she presented a cool exterior for her mother, her nerve endings sparked with discovery, barely able to remain relaxed beneath her heated skin.

Devi had believed Nicu's Living Ink would be her control and the norm. She had been wrong. She'd expanded both crystals to beach ball size, twisted and turned them around each other until she realized the main threads didn't match. Instead, the weakest connections were perfect replicas, though so numerous that she wasn't ready to map them so late in the day.

Between the heaviest and lightest strands, she found a third set that mostly matched but were often sidetracked by the more powerful strings. These correlated lines pulsed, a heartbeat within the very Ink of the tattoo. They were also the least prevalent, and she'd been able to sketch them for both samples, making notes for when they broke pattern to adjust around the thickest cables.

Veil energy. At first, Devi didn't believe it. She double checked her research on the barrier to confirm and minus the adjustments, they matched.

But how did they get barrier energy into their Ink? Why did Ember have more, and Nicu less? Did the different volumes of barrier magic within the tattoo even mean anything? Were the pair connected, or was this all chance? Had the Fae done this, or was it an anomaly of the Trimarked Child and Nicu, who had been present at her birth?

Devi wanted more samples. Maybe from Edan. Certainly from Branna. She would have to figure out a way to trade for them, or steal if she must, much as she had with Nicu. She salivated over the idea of all that data, and all she could learn about something so alien and intriguing.

In her excitement, and with no other data to study, Devi couldn't resist playing with the crystal. The magic was gorgeous, and she'd felt so content surrounded by it. She would have stayed for hours if her mother hadn't interrupted.

"Did you need something?" Devi asked.

"I... yes, I thought so, but if you've been Working most of the day, I can find someone else."

"I'm all right."

"Really, it's fine."

"Mom. I've been studying books and taking notes. I wouldn't mind another errand."

"It's late."

Devi crossed her arms. Her mom's sudden hesitation had little to do with the hour and more to do with the magic she'd walked in on.

"I know it's hard for you to wrap your head around what I can do, but I promise, the spell wasn't as taxing as it looked. In fact, I have energy to spare. Where would you like me to burn it?"

"Is that something you can teach?"

Devi huffed, frustrated her mother wouldn't get to the point.

"The true Earth talents should be able to do it, though we'd want to practice with flawed jewels. I expect a few will burst into dust until the skill is mastered."

"Hmm." Leona stared into space, fingering her gems. "And its application?"

"Ah." Devi touched the tip of her tongue to the edge of her teeth. That part would be more difficult, at least the way Devi used them. "I'm not sure," she hedged. "Perhaps… your scrying images could be as big as you needed…."

Leona smiled with the idea. "Well, all work and no play makes for a dull day. I suppose having fun with magic has its place."

"Like at Celebration," Devi agreed, and she unwrapped her arms. "Are you going to tell me what you need at any point?"

"Oh, yes. A patrol discovered an odd parting of energy, like a path had been cut along just that ribbon of space. The spell had no obvious purpose and has been very slow to return to normalcy. We are assuming it wasn't you?"

"It was not."

"The scouts seemed uneasy about it, said there was something odd but couldn't be specific. I can have anyone follow it, and will if you prefer. I hope you might be able to dissect it, figure out why it caused their discomfort."

Devi sucked in a deep breath. The coven didn't ask for her help often. As nice as it was to be needed, their current request did not settle well in her bones.

"You need someone to go right now?"

"Yes. In case it dissipates."

"What do you think it is?"

"I'm not sure," Leona said. "Since it's on our land, it likely rules out the Fae, but not necessarily. We need to understand the specifics of it before I ask them questions, anyway. They'll deny it either way, and we won't have any leverage unless we have proof. If it's one of us, we need to know who can cast that type of spell and why they would do so without someone in the coven knowing about it."

Leona pursed her lips and looked behind her toward the door where evening beams of late sunshine painted the floor. "Perhaps you should take a few archers with you, though. It's getting dark."

Devi grabbed her coat and followed her mom. Two scouts, Liam and Oriel, accompanied her through the forest. Witch-flame levitated around their knees, bright enough to light their path and not so high as to blind them. The previous party left willow-the-wisp markers, small fires Devi extinguished on their way along the trail.

Devi saw the disturbance first and stopped. Liam moved a few feet beyond her to check the path's safety, then shuddered with contact and jumped back.

"Found it," he announced.

"You can't see it?" she asked.

"You can?"

Devi waved him off, stepped up to the anomaly and dipped her fingertips in.

The edge was hot, the center cool, but not as cold as the night air around the rest of her body. The power didn't flow as suggested, but more likely parted, then became stagnant in the middle.

"A masking spell for unseen passage," she said. Difficult, worrying magic.

"What caused this?" Liam asked.

"Who did it? Can you figure it out?" Oriel asked.

"Not with the little evidence here." Devi traced the gap with her eyes toward the human neighborhood, realized with a start that it took a sharp turn a few feet to her right, angled toward No Man's Land.

"You two will have to dip a few fingers and trace it that way." She pointed to the left. "The path turns up here. I'll follow that leg. If you find anything, send for the nearest scouting party to join you. If you lose it, head back to the Circle and report to the High Priestess."

"We should stick together." Liam shuddered and Devi wondered with a half-smile if he was more concerned with sticking together, or in not having to touch the discomforting magic of the tracking spell.

"You are not my guards. If you want to find out what caused this, we have to track it. The creator is likely on one of either end. As I'm not interested in staying up all night, splitting up is the best option. Now, go."

The scouts hesitated, argued with scowls and quick eye movements over who would be the guide. Oriel pulled rank with a deep frown, then the two moved out.

Devi stepped through the cut with a shiver. The space had a weaker, though similar, repellant to No Man's Land, and the exact reason she chose this path for herself. No Man's Land was not her concern. What she didn't need was anyone, particularly an unknown, discovering her hidden place of power.

26

NICU

"I warned you not to run into anything."

Chase ambled into the moonlit clearing. His hand fit into the pockets of his elongated sweater without the need to bend elbows. "Nicu, do you mind releasing my tracking hound?"

Friends with Brandt, attached to Ember's side when last seen, Nicu was not inclined to release Aaron. He was interested in his appearance with Chase, however.

"He has ties to too many parts of this."

Chase frowned, his attention deliberately leveled at Nicu rather than on the boy he held.

"As do we all, but in Aaron's case, I'm thinking you might not have the entire story."

Nicu tilted his head, a silent demand for answers. Edan shifted beside him, breath pushed through his nose. So it was not Chase's knowledge alone. At least he did not have to trade Aaron for intel.

"The Child can manipulate the barrier," Edan said. "She pushed Brandt through last night after he attacked her."

Which is why Edan hadn't shared the information before. Here was the answer to a question Nicu had meant to ask hours ago after seeing her bruises, before he'd gotten side-tracked by Wist. The hybrid girl had taken care of Brandt herself in a way that did not allow Nicu to follow up.

Nicu released Aaron.

"Branna, attach to the human."

She melted out into view. Aaron jumped, then clenched his fists in an effort to control himself while Branna stepped next to and slightly behind him, as if she'd become his shadow.

"Nice trick," Chase responded to the female Fae. "Is that something I can learn?"

"Wizards are too colorful to blend in," Branna taunted, self-satisfaction curled on her lips.

"There's a compliment in there somewhere, but I'm more interested in what got Aaron off the hook."

"He knows I couldn't have brought Brandt back." Aaron rolled his shoulders, discomfort in the lines of his curved spine. He bounced on his toes, then winced and put a hand to the side of his jeans, dark and stiff with dried blood. Nicu scrutinized each movement, but only learned someone had injured the human. Words, then.

"Why are you with Chase?"

Aaron flinched away from Nicu's question, took it for the attack it was.

"I couldn't fight Brandt by myself, so I went to Chase."

There was more, a piece of information at the edge of observation.

"You have seen him?" Nicu asked.

"Yeah, and got stabbed in the leg for the trouble."

Nicu's blood chilled, stilled his movement and slowed his thoughts.

Stabbed. The impression of being cut open. The tear in the barrier.

"Look," Aaron continued. "I didn't know what he was about. I'm here to help Ember so if we could drop the debate and get to the part where we find her that would be —"

Nicu crowded Aaron against the nearest tree. Branna ghosted beside him, always the same distance from Aaron. Nicu tested for and tasted magic, jerked the lines of the power to him.

"For fade's sake!" Aaron shouted.

"Nicu, what are you—" Chase approached, but Edan stopped the Halfer.

"Silence," Nicu commanded, and searched the magic.

A weakening charm on Aaron's chest pulsed with his heartbeat and seemed to be supporting the human's depleted energy. It was Witch magic that had nothing to do with what Nicu looked for. He focus on the wound at Aaron's thigh, dug beneath the layers of Chase's healing without undoing the Work, shifted through the fibers.

Steel and blood.

Nicu fixed onto Aaron's angry gaze.

"Why are you here?"

"I am trying to help Ember." Each word concise in sincerity.

Nicu pressured Aaron with a forward tilt of his brow.

"Not your intent," he growled. "Your location."

Clarity smoothed the lines on Aaron's face. Satisfied he had made his point, Nicu allowed Aaron room to move. The human ruffled a hand through his curls, his focus cautious.

"This is where we found her." He pointed at the ground where Nicu had already determined the hybrid had rested. "Ember was there."

"We. You and Brandt."

Aaron's hands flew up, defensive.

"I swear I was not helping him."

"He had the knife with him." Nicu said, having determined Aaron was not an accomplice, but a source.

Aaron hesitated, and Nicu breathed through impatience.

"Yeah, he stabbed me right over there."

Nicu turned, pulled his sleeve above his elbow and called

forth the harnessing power of his Living Ink. He located the blood on the ground, captured and crushed a handful of the debris, let his tattoos rub against the magic they found within.

He stood, threw the leaves as he'd thrown the traces of Ember's power. Nicu used force of will to harness the bits into being, mindful not to lose them to the negative space. The cloud zipped around the clearing, mimicking Brandt's movements, then stopped at the edge of No Man's Land toward the Circle.

Hands clenched at his side, Nicu burned, turned his frustration to Chase who wavered for the first time that evening.

"I need Devi."

"Words I bet you wish I'd never heard." Devi sauntered through the forest, witchflame in hand. She jolted to a stop behind the floating mass of bloodied leaves before curling her lip and circling around it.

"By the way, Chase, how does he know you can contact me?" she asked with sweet venom.

Nicu did not allow the Halfer to answer. "Why are you here?"

Devi's hard stare lingered on Chase. He remained silent, long arms in low pockets, eyes on everyone except for Devi. Nicu noticed the flash in Devi's eyes the moment she decided to deal with him later.

"For someone who just asked for me, you don't seem happy with my arrival. I suppose your grumpiness comes from the fact that you lost your ward."

She spoke as if he'd misplaced something trivial, a barb meant to highlight the incompetence she imagined in him. A distraction. Nicu closed his eyes against the chaos of emotions, opened them with the control of his mind.

"What information do you have?"

"About Ember? Your losing her was just a guess. You should hide your feelings better if you want to keep secrets like that."

Devi sent a wind through the offending debris. Nicu stalked forward with a low rumble, warning against her casual use of magic against his own.

"Relax. You won't find her that way."

"Where?"

Devi pursed her lips. "That's not very polite."

"A trade, then." His words flew sharply off his tongue. "You followed a negative energy trail to get here, one cut into being."

The Witch angled her body toward him, witchflame raised for illumination.

"How do you know this?"

Because he did not have time, Nicu answered.

"Those fragments you brashly disbursed were not keyed to the girl but to the object hiding her and her assailant from you. A spelled knife. So I ask again. Where?"

"I get the blade." Devi's brazen negotiation reflected she understood the need to be quick, yet it caused Nicu to pause. Even in moments of urgency, agreements should always be handled with care.

"Under the same conditions as your research." He twisted a forearm, a physical indication that he referred to Ink. "And with disclosure of full knowledge."

Devi wavered, hesitant to promise something of unknown value. It was not long before she accepted the terms.

"The path's trajectory led toward the End of the World."

Nicu turned to find Aaron and Chase gone. Branna would be with them, assigned as a shadow. The negotiation delayed him, but no matter.

"Edan, permit Devi to attach herself to you."

"When did you learn so much about Witch magic?" Devi demanded, even as she prepared to cast the spell that would allow her to use Edan's speed as her own.

Nicu did not have time to answer. He left her behind.

27

SUSAN

*W*as that pounding in her head or from someone knocking?

Susan Lee sat up, blinked until she realized her house was dark and nothing was wrong with her sight.

"Ember?"

Soft, familiar night sounds convinced Susan there'd been no noise. She pulled the blanket up over her nose and sighed.

Up again, she stared at the door. It shook under the weight of a heavy fist. Her fingers trembled with something more than cold.

It was closing in on winter, but not too close since Ember hadn't hung the blankets yet.

But why was someone at her door? Why wasn't Ember rushing out to answer it, to put her small body between the outside world and Susan's wreckage? What was she supposed to do with the noise?

The person banged again. They weren't going away. Susan could ask them to come back when Ember got home. Make the pounding stop until Ember took care of it.

Susan struggled against the frigid temperature. She wrapped her long, warm afghan around her shoulders and shuffled in rubber soled house slippers she'd forgotten to take off earlier.

Good thing. Now her feet wouldn't get cold.

"Hello?" she called through the door, hoping she didn't have to open it.

A burst of new knocks sent Susan shuffling backward in surprise. What was going on?

Sharp fear parted Susan's cloudy mind. Ember was not here. Someone banged on her door. She remembered somebody told her Ember might be in trouble.

She rushed forward, yanked on the door and pressed herself onto the threshold, breath held.

No one on the stoop.

Susan's fingers curled into the crocheted gaps of her wool blanket. Her wide eyes tried to translate shadows into truth down the hill and to either side of her house. Empty.

Maybe Ember slept, and the noise had been an illusion in a broken mind. Susan retreated by inches. The fear she'd felt still monitored her movements, her heart not ready to close up if her daughter was in danger.

"It's time."

Susan's gasp burst so deep, her stomach cramped on the frost-tinged air. This voice haunted her nightmares and didn't belong in the waking world. She slammed the door on it.

"Ember," she tried again, her forehead pressed against the metal surface. She listened for any sign of movement from the closet where Ember slept, a room that barely worked now that she'd grown up, but had made perfect sense for a baby.

Perhaps that's why she hadn't come. She was a newborn tucked away in the crate Susan had scrounged, swaddled in an old sweater against the night. That would be why the blankets weren't on the walls yet, because Ember wasn't old enough to hang them.

The nightmare voice crawled through Susan's brain, taking hold in the depths. Her arm wrapped around her middle. Was it big? Still fat with child? Is that why she'd heard him? Had every moment she believed she'd been away from him been the dream? Now she was awake, and he was ready to take her?

Tears filled Susan's hollowed cheeks. Her knees struck the floor with the weight of fear, and the heaviness of memories.

⑅

Another contraction ignited across Susan's belly, tightened every stretch of skin, reached around to twist into a knot at the base of her spine. She couldn't breathe, each function frozen with the clenching of her womb as if a hot ember tried to burn through her.

Susan sat on a dirty couch in the middle of the abandoned maintenance unit dressed in a polyester maxi dress not meant for pregnancy, and stretched to its limits.

She'd been here for weeks, rarely left except to steal food from the Witches' gardens when the moon shone bright enough to help find her way. The moment her family had found out she was pregnant with a Wizard's baby, they'd beat her until she fled the house. They had tossed her things out of her second-story window. She collected those at night, handfuls at a time, until they realized what she was doing and burned the rest before she claimed it.

The contraction eased. Her tears redoubled. She tried not to reflect on where she was, tried not to imagine having to give birth in this filth.

There was nowhere to go. Other girls had gotten pregnant by mages. Some were protected by their family, some kicked out like her. Some kept the child. Sometimes the infant disappeared. Susan knew - hoped - they were in Trifecta somewhere, but she'd never been able to find where.

The door burst open. She squeezed her eyes shut, didn't want to see him, or to acknowledge the shadow in her mind. She pulled her knees up, hid her belly from him.

"It's time."

A Wizard. Someone she didn't trust but had been forced to rely on when he'd been the only person to offer help. Disgust of the mages kept her away at the beginning. Desperation led her to agree. Now he hauled her up without care and ordered her through the door, out into the blinding sunshine.

He had a way of moving through space that shortened any distance. Susan fought the wave of dizziness with each step. Nausea rolled in between the monstrous cramping. His frustration burned through her every time a contraction made them stop. His breath was a curse when her water broke and soaked her skirt.

"Susan!" The shout suggested he'd called her name a few times. He shifted her so her head fell back, but she kept her gaze low, stared at his thin lips. "Are you listening?"

She hummed her awareness.

"This part you will have to do on your own, do you understand?"

"W-what? How could I—"

"We need all three powers to help break the curse. You are going to visit the third. And I have to leave."

"You're abandoning me with this!"

"What did you expect?"

"For you to destroy the barrier! For the mages to go home! For everything to be normal again!"

"I see patience is not your virtue." He forced her feet to move as he shifted her from his body and sent a curled lip glare at the damp spot she'd left on his coat. "Find some."

A wicked knife sliced a shallow gash across her bicep. His eyes glistened as if he expected thanks for a gift. He thrust her from him with a burst of muscle and magic.

Susan reached for him as she stumbled backward. She was still on his fast track path. Each single step took her as far away as ten. Then he was gone.

She landed hard. The impact forced a rough contraction

through her, from spine to stomach and into the bones of her pelvis. She screamed and clawed at the dirt beneath her, desperate to grasp something, to find anything sturdy enough to help brace herself.

"What in the realms….?" Two faces appeared before her wet vision. Every hair in place, clothes well tailored with no accessory to get in the way.

He'd thrown her onto Fae land. Terror clenched her heart as surely as the contractions held the rest of her body hostage. She turned to crawl away, hoped it was the right direction, screamed when the agony penetrated her hips.

"Go alert the council," one of the Fae ordered.

"Thyia, are you sure?"

"Quickly. I'll keep your son." Thyia dropped to her knees even though she wore a knee length dress, perfectly tailored around her own, full-bellied pregnancy. She guided Susan's shoulders flat against the ground with gentle, insistent pressure, then rubbed the domed surface of Susan's abdomen.

The Fae woman gasped at the touch, gripped her own stomach as pain radiated through her.

Susan cried out. The strain became too much to bear, and she pushed. Thyia recovered and shifted lower along Susan's body, pressed her gown up and stripped off her underwear.

Then the Fae collapsed on her own shriek. Susan twisted, saw blood flow past the hem of Thyia's summer dress. Dark, disbelieving eyes accused Susan.

"What have you done to me? What have you brought here?"

"H-he forced me," Susan gasped, then growled. Her shout blended into Thyia's scream.

In concert, two babies cried.

Footsteps added beat to the song, then stumbled to a stop. Susan struggled against the continued cramps to look up and see that which had torn her apart.

There, between the mothers sat a two-year-old boy covered

in muck, his eyes a chocolate brown full of warmth for the babies. He seized the foot of one, the arm of Susan's, and pulled them to his sides like dolls. Thyia lay with a slow, tired lowering of lashes, then stilled.

"No." The deep bass of the word was a command of revulsion so deep it drew Susan in. A male Fae looked on in horror, his long white locs still swaying with his abrupt stop.

Susan did not understand his words, but she saw the movement on his hands. Ink a shade darker than his skin, V's connected with each leg to the ones above, patterned and spaced like scales or armor. A Fae was casting a spell. It would be against her daughter.

A daughter the wicked Wizard had left to her. Not his. Not theirs. Hers.

Pleasant heat flushed beneath the pain, and she desperately wanted to hold the source of that comforting warmth. Her little Ember.

She pushed up to fall back down, another contraction ripped through, her body eager to finish the birth as a flash burst throughout the clearing with the heavy sound of lightning splitting air.

One baby stopped bawling. Susan's breath ground out. Her heartbeat redoubled with life when she saw it was her newborn who still keened, the other as limp as her mother.

The toddler screamed.

Susan blinked through her tears, focused through the blur to see him hug the babies, head bowed. He scrunched his face in concentration and air wavered around him as if superheated, though he didn't have tattoos to betray his magic.

The second baby regained her breath, stuttered into a frightened cry. The transparent, blurry wave arched toward the man who cast it. His Ink gathered in palms thrust out as a shield against his own spell.

He threw the power away as the Wizard had thrown Susan, only with less intent. The energy hit the woman who had gone for help. Her skin paled, and she collapsed to the ground.

"Mama?" The boy opened eyes no longer the color of dark chocolate. They had lightened and sharpened into amber glass. He looked at the small girls next to him, left the babies he saved for the mother he would never know again.

More footsteps thundered their way, Fae scouts she'd seen as they hunted, others dressed like the man, wrapped in heavy, patterned wool.

"Wist. What is this?" one woman asked.

"An aberration I could not stop. I tried, and it backfired--" the Fae choked on the words, gestured toward the dead bodies. The newly arrived Fae woman recoiled, horror on her face.

"You dared to use High Magic?" she demanded.

The grieving Fae cleared his throat with a pained, angry growl. "It was necessary! Do you not sense the child's blood?"

The woman narrowed her eyes, then hissed and she turned away from the scene.

Exhausted, Susan curled over the cramps in her stomach. Gentle echos let her know she was done. She scrambled at the ground, gripped her daughter and pulled her from the horror of gore and dirt, the warmth of her baby fighting against the chill of fear.

Tears cut down Susan's cheeks. She wished she'd stayed in that dusty shelter, wished she'd cared earlier about the protection of herself and her newborn Ember.

"Bring them to Center," Wist ordered. "There is nothing else to do. We shall bind the child."

}I{

They had forced magic on Susan. Their magic scarred Ember. Susan had stumbled back into the place she would call home, a tattooed baby in her arms. The Wizard never visited again.

But she'd heard him tonight.

"No."

Susan gripped the roots of her hair, pulled hard enough until the pain helped her separate what was inside her head and what was not.

That had been the dream. The dream of knocking. The dream of his voice.

Magic had no place here. She'd forbidden it. It only dared to appear while she slept.

Knock knock knock.

Sobs rattled through Susan's ribs. She'd felt it, the vibration against her forehead.

"It's time."

His words. Muffled through the door. Or through time. She wasn't sure anymore.

Susan opened the door, chin high, bottom lip quivering.

Empty.

Except the shadows moved.

Down the slope, the shape of a man crossed the road and disappeared into the tree line.

She gripped the knob in one hand, the blanket held at her neck. It could be a trick of the moon or some teenager out playing tricks. Maybe her nightmares had somehow left her head.

Susan stepped out onto the concrete steps. She fought queasiness at the prospect of this hide and seek game, a game that could be entirely in her mind.

Only one way to find out.

28

EMBER

*E*mber crashed to the ground for the twenty-seventh time. Her shoulder popped when Brandt hauled her to her feet and glared at her for slowing them down.

"Can't you walk?"

Ember grit her teeth. "Yeah, I can even run or sneak away from jerks trying to catch me after I slam their faces into cars."

"Then fading do it. We don't have all night." Brandt didn't rise to the bait. This timeline might actually be important. Whatever 'business' he had with her had to finish before this creepy mage showed up.

"Sure, no problem. Tell you what. Free my hands and I'll jump right to your tune."

Brandt growled and shoved her forward. Ember yelped when her foot landed lower than expected, balance lost, and she toppled down a hill. She groaned with pain, rolled to a stop, too stunned to scramble away before Brandt jogged to her side.

"Good hustle, mutt, and I didn't even have to untie you."

Blood tasted bitter. Her tongue swelled from the cut of her teeth. She spat into the rubble. Brandt hoisted her up. The torture in her shoulder weakened her resolve, and she cried out.

"Get your feet under you, damn it," he grunted when she slipped.

Well, getting badly injured would slow them further. Ember just wished Brandt had gotten the twisted ankle instead.

Brandt forced her to march on. They cut through yards. Brandt cursed whenever he had to find a way around a fence, Ember tied up and too wounded to climb over. Her favorite were the brief stretches of street they got to cross. The flat, even surfaces didn't hide garden tools, raised roots or other nighttime traps.

When they turned to walk along a street instead of across it, Ember heaved her head up. She recognized one of the rare sections of maintained pavement where trees grew on each side. The last time she'd been here, cars had lined the road and faced the edge.

Brandt released her near the boundary. She plunged to the ground, let him think he'd been her sole support as he approached the invisible wall. Ember slid backward toward the shoulder, watched Brandt raise his hands with intimate knowledge of where the barrier began. One fist, one knife, and he tapped as softly as a prayer.

"It's almost over," he declared.

He turned to see her dig her feet into the dirt and run up the slight rise to the woods.

Brandt's shout sent a rush of frightened energy to her legs. She lowered her head, desperate to find a place to hide amongst the trees. His footsteps were too loud. She dropped and rolled, stopped moving at the bottom of a wide redwood. Stayed still and held her breath.

He passed her, vibrating in rage. Ember trembled, shock convulsed through her muscles, threatened her stomach.

Then he was back, flashlight bright, and found her.

Brandt left behind any gentleness. He hauled her up with his fist in the roots of her hair. She sobbed as he forced her forward.

"All this time and you could have ended it. But I'll be the one, and everyone will know it tomorrow."

Ember gasped, desperate to regain control, needed to get away, to delay. Brandt's helper might come soon. There was a chance he wouldn't be evil. She swallowed her pain, bowed her head. Blood thumped behind her closed eyes, and she clenched her teeth against the acidic rise of nausea.

"I've had a day without the damn Fae spell blocking my brain to think about this," Brandt panted. "Obviously, you want us all trapped here, but I wondered why you would stay. I mean, you get to watch us suffer, to force us to pretend we can work together with the mages, but then I thought, well, maybe you can't keep the bubble up if you're not in it, too."

Like a sack of flour, Brandt hefted Ember forward, swung her until her body cracked against impenetrable air.

"Brandt," she wheezed. "Brandt, I can't do what you're asking. I'm not—"

"Yes you can! I've seen you do it, if you remember." He stomped away from her, swiped sweat from his brow. "I brought you here so your outsider friends won't be close enough to stop this. Not before I watch you shatter every inch of this fading dome."

The last dredges of Ember's energy poured out in waves of horror.

"I cannot."

"Damn it, stop telling me that! You did it. You do it. You did it to me!"

"Yes." She swallowed past her dry, swollen tongue. "One person, one small door."

"Make it bigger. An arch, whatever."

"Even if I could, it would close in seconds. Too fast for a car to pass."

Brandt stared at her, not comprehending and certainly not believing. His fingers adjusted along the wooden handle of his knife as he struggled to figure out why she hadn't done what he wanted.

"You tossed me out."

"It took less than a second. Think about it. You tried to return immediately, remember?"

"Because you closed it."

Hot tears pricked Ember's eyes when he raised the knife toward her face.

"Brandt, please. It doesn't work that way. Believe me."

His lips curled in a sneer. He approached with a speed too fast for her bruised brain to comprehend, lifted her rag doll body.

"Or I've been too nice and you don't get it." He shoved her against the barrier, her cheek flattened and her lungs compressed with his weight against her back. His left hand tangled in her hair, pressured her bones onto the unforgiving surface. Once she was secure, he sliced through the ropes, not taking caution with her skin and cut into the base of her palms.

Ember's hands hung by her sides, useless pendulums he expected her to use.

"Do it now, mutt. Open the damned door. We'll see then how big you can make it, how long it will stay. Or I'll just stick this knife right in your throat. Maybe killing you is the real answer."

The effort to turn her palms against the barrier proved monumental. Her fingertips slipped against the energy. Power crackled, then sputtered out. She bared her teeth and urged strength into fingers numb from being tied up, fallen on, crushed.

Tap tap tap.

Tap tap. Tap.

Nothing.

Her body shuddered with the failure, with her last chance

to manage a miracle that put them on separate sides once again.

"I can't." Her voice broke. Brandt pulled on her hair to lift her chin.

Tears coated Ember's cheeks. She didn't even have the strength to flinch when the weapon's point touched the ridge of her throat.

"Please," she begged.

"Have it your way."

Brandt pulled the knife away, twisted his torso for leverage. Vibrations shattered through her body, blood flared in her veins. Life pulsed in heartbeats at the cut in her brow, the raw skin at her wrists, a wrenching reminder of the life he would take. Blue sparks lit behind her eyelids and she felt an unnatural warmth wrap around her, a poor imitation of comfort.

With a solid swing, Brandt thrust the blade toward her neck.

Ember's singular essence flared and exploded into sapphire shards.

29

NICU

The human and Halfer traveled the road, thought it the fastest path. Perhaps for them.

Nicu cut straight through the yards of houses, leveraged every advantage he owned. He trampled grass, ran across roads. His strength lent ease to small garden fences. Taller privacy boards took only a moment to vault. The ability to sense terrain and see through the dark kept his feet light and his path unhindered.

He broke the tree line, and the world stopped.

Ember, only partially visible from behind Brandt's larger form. Tears gleamed on her cheeks, eyes closed against the blade threatening her skin.

Wist had ordered Nicu to contain chaos.

Nicu lifted his hands beneath his braids. Fingers pinched the thin metal of the Trimark medallion, one hand on the wing, the other on the pentacle.

The Ternate should not be allowed to bring unforeseen changes.

Brandt pulled back the knife. The threat increased with its distance.

Nicu's entire purpose was to keep the hybrid girl contained and secure.

Terraborn, Nicu knew control was not always the answer.

He brushed the pendant. The wing fluttered on a hidden seam.

Blue energy blinded Nicu.

Brandt shouted in pained surprise.

Behind him, Branna screamed. The tie that bound them strained in response to his manipulation of the talisman. The medallion wanted to forge a new link between him and Ember, sacrificing the Fae-spelled bond between himself and Branna. Nicu's heart slammed.

He could not do this, not to Branna. It was not like him to be so brash. He needed to refocus. Breathe.

He snapped the Trimark closed.

He ran despite being blinded by the bright flash of light that corresponded with his slip in judgement and rushed onward to the last place he'd seen Ember Lee. With each step, his vision cleared, and the night filled in.

A bolt of electricity split the sky, rain gushed with a peal of resonating thunder.

Brandt, less than a yard from Ember, scanned the ground for something lost as he shuffled and kicked with his feet. The knife.

Lightning flashed again, but not from the dark clouds above. The blue streams of power radiated from Ember. Nicu skid to a stop. His heartbeat slowed, his breathing stuttered.

"What in the realms is that?" Devi demanded, pulled forward by Edan who looked on with open amazement.

Ember hung suspended. Her arms at her side, hair spread in a haphazard arch. Sapphire light flowed into and from her body, condensed into white at her chest.

"Close your eyes," Nicu warned. Another shot of lightning flared through the night, lit upon each freezing raindrop, illu-minated the shape of the dome. Nicu felt the echo of concentrated power in his own blood, a gentle fizzle compared to the raw energy running through Ember.

"Oh, gods." Devi wrenched herself away from Edan and hurried toward Ember. Brandt turned on the Witch, threw an arm out to catch her across the chest. Devi hit the ground hard, kicked at Brandt's legs.

"Help Devi." Chase shoved Aaron past Nicu. "I will get him."

"He's my fault."

"Exactly."

Aaron groaned in frustration, then nodded. He dropped back, waited for Chase to face Brandt. A full body thrust moved the human away from the others. Chase swept a leg, but Brandt held him close, used Chase's own weight to hold him up. Brandt smashed his brow into Chase's cheekbone and gained momentum to throw a jab into the Halfer's gut. Chase turned with it, got his elbow up and into Brandt's nose, took advantage of the bend forward to propel a knee into his ribs.

"What do we do?" Edan's words were low in Nicu's ear. The Fae watched from the side of the road. Branna limped up between them.

"Branna. Tell me."

Nicu remained still because Brandt was not his responsibility. He did not engage because the barrier was not in danger, sporadic in energy as it was. He did not contain stray magic because the weather itself would mask the actions here from the rest of Trifecta, beings across the city hiding from the intense autumn thunderstorm.

He refused to allow the hybrid girl out of his sight, encased as she was in a pocket of the brilliant webbing of the barrier.

Had it worked? Had a flicker of the medallion been enough to save her? Or had his hesitation over Branna's pain caused him to fail?

"Tell me," he ordered again. Branna shook her head, her hands raised in his peripheral.

"It's too bright. I can't see."

"Ask the spirits! Is there one more among them?" Uncontrolled breath, he demanded Branna tell him if the hybrid girl lived in the barrier, or if she'd perished in the flood of power.

"They're gone, they don't like it here—"

"Nicu!" Devi called out over the battles of man and nature. Her glare accused, her body stiff with outrage. "Get over here!"

He would have to find out for himself. Nicu's breath failed him.

Nicu's steps took him from natural earth to solid asphalt. He walked as if the events were not urgent, as if he had time. He reached the double yellow line at the center, the very marker that led to Ember's form.

Devi grasped his wrist and directed him forward, pulled him in, thrust him into proximity.

"Nicu," Chase called in warning. Edan ran past, took the blow Brandt had meant for Nicu.

Devi jabbed Nicu's chest, insisting on his attention as if they hadn't been in danger of attack, as if what happened before them was more urgent.

And at that moment, Nicu understood.

Ember was alive.

Nicu breathed.

"You have to free her," Devi said.

"How?"

"Both of your tattoos are laced with Veil energy. For now, I assume that isn't the same for all Fae Ink. To be safe, it has to be you."

Nicu raised a hand. Devi slammed it back. "You can't touch that power," she snarled. "It's raw, truly elemental."

Nicu curled his lip. There was no need to give an order, Devi far ahead of him.

"Use your tattoos. They are made from the same Ink, but hers has a different magical structure."

"Hers is binding."

"Apply the Life in your Ink to free hers. The Veil energy should also be freed, and allow her to get out."

Nicu recoiled, denial thrust into his core. Unbind the Trimarked Child. He thought of her hands sparking with magic, power he'd disbursed into the world.

"Even if that were possible, this would be her norm," he snarled. "She cannot control herself."

"You haven't given her a chance."

Devi didn't understand. She hadn't seen Ember flare, or the fear and denial in the hybrid girl's eyes. A Witch could not comprehend that some magic was best left untapped. Magic he had almost wielded himself, he was reminded, as the skin at his neck itched against the weight of the Trimark.

He glanced at Branna, slumped onto the ground. He would not try the medallion again, not until he understood her connection to it. Behind him, Edan had Brandt well secured. Chase and Aaron stood by just in case. They were not Nicu's concern.

Nicu studied Ember, closed his eyes when he sensed the next flash ready to break. His tattoos twitched. He'd worked far too hard to lose the girl now.

Devi might be right, though not in the way she expected.

Nicu's fingers flexed. He stepped closer to Ember, brushed off Devi's attempt to restrain him.

She did not understand.

Nicu directed power and order. Ink drew forward on his body, crawled down his arms, hair stood on end in response to the movement. Tattoos collected into his palms, saturated the skin over his torso and down the front of his thighs, ready to receive.

This was what made him different. Nicu could not call on magic itself. He had to steal it.

He would take hers.

Ember hung suspended in the barrier, but his height was

greater. His feet remained on the ground as Nicu fit his chest to Ember's back, lowered his hands upon hers, pressed his cheek to her temple, but it was not her he touched. The power of the Veil had become a shell over and around her, absorbed her form as if she were another stretch of the invisible shield.

Yours is mine.

His tattoos swirled at the contact, reached for the resonating pull of barrier energy mixed with Ink in the hybrid girl's body. The Ink dipped onto the smooth energy with tiny spikes of their own power, drunk and full within seconds. Ember's essence pushed out the particles of magic like beads of sweat. Nicu gripped them with force of will through the channel of his Living Ink and urged the power to leave her, to move along, nourish the barrier, bolster the storm.

His fingertips brushed hers. He transferred more out and away. The soft strands of her hair caressed his cheek. The proof of her life added strength to his beating heart.

"Nicu!"

Edan's deep shout commanded Nicu's focus outward for an instant, enough loss of focus for the shell to move from around them to between them. It pushed him away and took Ember with it. The wind carried the sound of a freight train. Thunder quaked the earth.

He did not have time for this.

Nicu compelled the energy with a wave of command until their bodies were once more in the same space. He braced himself against the interior surface, demanded his power seize Ember, and keep the energies from dividing them.

Distance grew in front of Ember. Every physical and metaphysical muscle strained within Nicu's being. He wrapped an arm around her ribs once the gap was large enough, curved his back against the cocoon.

The surrounding power did not have strands to grab or weave. It did not have tiny pieces to collect in his palms. This energy was fluid, but it resisted movement.

A deep breath and he trembled, weakened. The energy oozed and pushed into the fissures between their bodies, pulling Ember away from him.

"No." The small sound conveyed the strength of his resolve, added vitality to his form, enforced his command of magic and imposed his will.

Power surged into his tattoos. Skin pulled as if pinched by thousands of tiny vices. The Living Ink responded to his commands, ripped from his pores to reach beyond, to enfold Ember's energy despite the overwhelming efficiency of the barrier. The Ink floated between them, found her exposed flesh, and gripped.

Nicu drove their bodies out, twisted within the gap until he beat the power back, until it was his strength surrounding her body, freeing them both from the fusion.

Wintery rain steamed off him. His chest heaved in the fresh air. Ink settled back into place. He cradled Ember on his lap, his torso bent over to protect her from the rain as his spirit cracked at the edges, all because of this small girl, this hybrid child.

Because now he had moved past understanding. Now he knew. Beyond doubt, Ember Lee had the power to unmake the world.

30

EMBER

*W*et drops stained Ember's face.

Was someone crying? Her eyes cracked open to the grey sky, then she relaxed and closed them again. Just the rain.

"Ember, wake up."

Nicu. A heavy sigh opened her chest. Was he here for her? Time to endure the Fae for being born unlucky.

Yet, she could not move her body, and it wasn't because she didn't want to.

"If you would let me closer, I could heal her." Devi enunciated with feigned restraint.

Had the Fae already found her? Maybe she'd forgotten who hurt her — Brandt.

Ember gasped, struggled against the arms that held her, needed to escape the press of him. The pitted asphalt bit into her palms. She scrambled on hands and knees to turn and confront her captor.

Golden eyes stared at her with heavy lids. He released her, so not Brandt. Rain blurred her vision. She blinked it clear, patted soaked strands of hair off her face and looked again.

Nicu.

Someone touched her shoulder. She jerked aside, flinched from the bright curls before she recognized Devi.

Then the worst person of all came into view. Wrapped in a sodden, knit-stretched afghan, her mom ran over the mud, crashed into the puddles of the road.

"You're alive," Susan breathed, hands shook as she reached toward her daughter.

"How did you get here?" Ember asked. "Why aren't you home?"

As Ember watched, relief turned to anger. The wet of tears became a gloss. "You chose him, I see. You chose magic. Fine. Fine. Fine! Do not come back." Vitriol melted into a sob and Susan twisted her body away, covered her face with a skeletal hand. "Please, Ember, do not bring that into my house."

"Mom." Ember reached, wanting to explain she hadn't done it on purpose, to swear she'd tried to stay away from the magic, but Susan lurched to her feet and shook her head. Ember lost her voice and her heart broke. She could only watch as her mother withdrew, distantly registered when Nicu sent Branna to follow.

Devi's warm magic tingled across Branna's skin. She shuddered and pushed the Witch's hand away.

"Too much."

"It's a healing spell. It barely takes any power."

"Leave her be. She is still overwhelmed with energy." Nicu stood over them. Ember looked up. The rain softened. His face betrayed nothing. Ember squirmed, not familiar with a lack of reaction. Anger, frustration, commanding, yes. A placid Nicu was new. She didn't know what it meant.

A different argument tugged at the edge of Ember's attention. Partial relief scattered through her when she saw Brandt on his knees with a length of rope around his wrists. Chase and Aaron pinned him.

"Are you sure you got him this time?" Edan's tone was dry. Aaron nodded, his eyes as flat as Nicu's, though his lips bent downward, his face turned away. So he'd gone for help after all, made the choice Brandt didn't think he would.

Edan left the three behind and approached Nicu. "Someone let him in."

"And gave him a knife," Devi said. "One I have not found." Her glare held Nicu responsible for the loss. He ignored her and answered Edan.

"Your spies are still silent."

Edan nodded, a flicker of concern softened his mouth.

"If this intruder had gotten to them, or if there are more outsiders working toward infiltrating Trifecta, we should know," Edan warned.

Nicu looked from the barrier to Devi. "You will have the knife, if found," he assured her. "Do you want Brandt?"

Devi's eyes lit devilishly onto the human. "Yes, but Nicu, why such a wonderful gift?"

"Silence."

Thanks to her lesson, Ember recognized the negotiation. Devi sauntered over for her prize, the terms agreed upon.

"Do you mind helping with transportation?" she asked Chase and Aaron.

"Just you wait, just you wait until the wizard gets here--" Brandt yelled as Chase and Aaron hauled him up to his feet. Devi twisted her wrist through the air, raised two fingers to his mouth, and his voice fell silent. Brandt struggled against the hands that gripped him, tried to kick his legs only to be dragged. His vicious snarl thrust toward Ember and Chase punched him in the side of the head to get him to look away.

With everyone else gone, Nicu turned to Ember, parted his lips, but was stopped when Edan placed a hand on his shoulder.

"Her agreement is with me." Ember's heart stuttered. Humans would call that a lie. Fae call it a chosen truth. Regardless, it worked. Nicu stepped aside to let Edan pass.

"Ready?" Edan asked.

"Is it safe?" Would she survive this time? Would the barrier try to hold her again? Would she explode in the end like she'd thought happened at the beginning when Brandt's anger had almost been her death? Would Nicu take her to the Fae after, or did her bargain protect her?

"It is safe, little hybrid," Nicu said. Whatever it meant, he was her constant. She believed him so completely that belief spread to her unasked questions.

With a shudder, Ember pushed herself to her feet. Trembling fingers reached forward to tap tap tap.

"Now," she whispered, feeling the smooth opening appear before her. The breeze in her face held an unfamiliar taste and brought a stimulating sensation to the depths of her lungs.

Edan disappeared from view before the barrier closed. Ember and Nicu stood side by side in the rain's soft whisper.

Without looking at him, she walked up the hill. He, of course, walked with her anyway.

"You cannot return home."

Ember's huff might be called a laugh, except it held no humor or heart. "Yeah. I got that part."

"It will not be safe for you."

"Now this is starting to sound familiar." Blood drained from her cheeks.

"I'm—"

"No. No apologies and absolutely no more promises."

Nicu paused.

"No. We've had enough of those," he murmured.

They'd had all of one, so exactly the correct assessment.

"Goodnight, Nicu." A dismissal. She expected him to argue. Instead, he became another shadow. Of course, Ember knew shadows never really went away.

Ember walked along the road, arms wrapped around to steady the wet chill, tired and numb. It wasn't until her feet crunched across gravel that she realized what she'd done.

She'd gone home. She wondered if she could slip in, if

Susan's vacillating mind might have forgotten she'd kicked her daughter out.

Except there was a blanket wrapped into a bag in the grass outside the front door. She stared at it, sucked in the cold and lifted her face to the rain.

"Leave it."

"What are you doing here?" she asked in a whisper, not wanting an audience while she discovered how deep her despair would drill into her bones.

"I dropped Aaron off, saw you on the road."

Aaron, her unexpected... unexpected. "How is he?"

"He's fine. He about collapsed at the Circle."

"What?" She gasped.

"The Witches gave him some concoction that will make him sleep for 24 hours while he replenishes his blood, then he'll wake up, charming as ever. What about you?"

Ember shrugged, stared at the wet mess on the lawn.

"Did you come to get some stuff?" Chase's voice was delicate in her ears, on her spirit. She turned with caution, though she had no words in the face of his soft tone.

"I'll get you more," he said. "Something less.... wet."

The laugh that punched through her broke through the pain, brought a sliver of light into her thoughts.

"And what will that cost me?" Her lips twisted with the familiar comfort of the question.

"You were the only one who demanded a price." Ember startled, her eyes wide on Chase, his hair plastered to his cheeks by the rain. He looped his arms around her shoulders.

It was a hug.

It was amazing.

Ember leaned in, shuddered with relief, shivered in the cold.

"Come on." He shifted to her side and kept his arm draped over her shoulders. "No reason to survive a magical storm only to die in a real one."

EPILOGUE
BRANDT

*B*randt's head hurt. The damn gnomes had done a number on him while they dragged him to some weird chain-link fence cell, one in a line against an outer wall of a warehouse they'd stolen after the Fade. He'd shaken the door half-heartedly. He didn't have enough energy to escape.

His body felt starved for air, but he knew better than to draw in a deep breath after an earlier try nearly had him blacking out. That damn Halfer was almost as tough as Brandt's old man. The gnomes had promised a healer. They had left the timeline to the imagination. Whatever. He could handle this. He'd had cracked ribs before and they were a bitch, but they weren't life threatening. For now, he needed to rest and bide his time.

Clipped footsteps filled the concrete expanse of the warehouse. Brandt grunted at the tall man topped with a bowed hat. A chuckle had him hissing in pain a moment later.

"Damn, it's good to see you," he told the Wizard who'd helped him once before. The weird guy remained silent as he approached the enclosure. He'd buttoned his long coat up this time, hands rested in his pockets as he looked at the crumpled mess Brandt made. "You're here to get me out, right?"

Tristan pulled a hand out of his pocket, waved it across his body with a few muttered words, and the cage door sprang open. Brandt tried to stand, groaned with the pain.

"No need to get up." Tristan stepped into the cell and looked down his sharp nose. "That was quite a scene back there."

"So you were there? But didn't come?" Brandt swallowed a painful lump as the Wizard simply stared. Maybe the guy hadn't intervened in case Brandt's plan worked, but then things got too crazy. Brandt didn't have the energy to fight about it right now, though. Once out and healed up a bit, they two could have a talk about setting some rules in this partnership. "Yeah, sorry about that. That bitch wouldn't break the barrier."

Tristan angled forward, his coat tight where it caught at the bend of his hips. It was the unnatural curl of his usually straight lips that sent a cold shaft of fear through Brandt's chest.

"Of course not, stupid boy."

Thin talon-like fingers gripped deep into Brandt's arms, lifted his broken body. Brandt cried out into the warehouse, the echo cut short, lost between one of the Wizard's steps and another.

Brandt dropped onto the forest floor. He scrambled back, the pain in his bones nothing compared to the panic that pulsed through his blood.

"Y-you got me out?" Yet the menacing form above him did not seem in the mood to assist. "So—so you still need my help? For your big plan."

"I wondered if you paid attention. But no, you have played your part. Well, most of it."

Those long fingers slipped open the top few buttons of his heavy coat, dipped into a breast pocket within and pulled out a small, closed pinecone. Brandt squinted, his fear stuttered under his confusion.

"What do you mean?"

"Your human blood is unique, tied to this land. Born in Trifecta after the Fade, trapped by the convergence, mingled every day of your life with the magics of human, Witch and Fae. Power that allowed me to carve our way through the barrier, if you recall."

Brandt folded his fingers over the scabbed line across his forearm. "You need more blood?"

"Of a sort." Tristan tilted forward, eased Brandt into the damp dirt. The light touch held Brandt with the weight of magic.

"What the hell are you doing?"

"This could have been painless," words murmured as if in confession. "But the truth is, I don't want it to be. You made a grave mistake when you attacked what's mine."

"What are yo--" Brandt choked on the word, on the realization he would not escape this one, not this time.

Tristan coaxed the hard shell of seeds into the soft flesh just below the junction of Brandt's ribs until the seed cut deep into his gut. Heat radiated through him, torched each nerve ending. He wanted to arch up, to push against the source, but his body sunk, his lungs clogged with the surge of roots. His blood ran into the dirt that swallowed him whole.

The weight of the sapling pressed him down even as new growth shot upward, outward. The trunk thickened, the branches punched out, narrowed, weighted with dark green needles as the tree rose into the sky and took every second of Brandt's years on Terra as its own.

ACKNOWLEDGMENTS

This book took so long to write, yet I truly feel it's come at the right time. The team I have around me now is who made this possible. I didn't have this kind of support in the past, which goes to show that the road to success is never traveled by only two feet.

My husband came into my life when I needed him the most. Twice. The first time, he helped me find the courage to go out into the world as a young woman, travel across the country for school, because he'd traveled the world to do the same. We lost contact for years, and then he returned, like magic, when I was the most broken. He's been with me ever since, cheering me on, supporting me through in my slumps, always reminding me that even if I only take one step, I'm still moving forward.

My kids are, honest to goodness, the littlest people in my life and my biggest cheerleaders. They celebrated with me over word counts, chapter completions, number of pages marked with the red pen, getting to write the end, hiring an editor ... all of it. They were there, jumping up and down and giving me hugs. Some days, it was those little celebrations that got me through that day's goal, making this book, on this timeline, possible.

The team I've collected have helped polish the story to a shine. Leigha, with me since first grade and through some of life's worst moments. She's always willing to read my stories, even when I had a habit of not finishing any of them. She was, and is, always there, asking for the next one.

Nicole, someone I met when I attempted my first blog. Her desire to work hard toward her goals has inspired me to go for mine, and I'm so thankful she's stuck around when I ducked out for a few years.

Eneida taught me to go outside my comfort zones, whether it's travel to rural Mexico, climbing a mountain or repelling through a canyon. The courage her adventures taught me led to the courage to finally make my work public.

Whitney of Wit & Travesty, has been incredibly supportive. Her developmental edits helped plug holes, answer questions, and smooth everything out in the end. I'm so glad I found her via Instagram.

Natalie from Original Book Cover Design / 4 Step Studio came in at just the right moment, not only to create beautiful book covers, but also became an unexpected and much needed mentor. Her help offered a boost of confidence when I might have otherwise taken a step back.

And then there's the writing community. Self-pub, newly published, small printer authors, who have guided me whether they knew it or not. A constant ghost on discussion threads, on Twitter, Instagram and Facebook, I learned so much from people far braver than I who were willing to ask the questions, and those who were kind and selfless enough to answer.

Thank you to all of you who took a chance on me, followed me on social media, joined my newsletter, put up with my awkward attempts to figure it all out at the beginning. And thank you, very, very much, for everyone who takes this story into their own minds, and makes it a little part of themselves.

ABOUT THE AUTHOR

CK Sorens is the pen name of Carrie Sorensen. Carrie lives in the Bay Area of California with her husband, Kristoffer, their three sons, and their dog, Pippin. She enjoys days at the beach, day hikes, and sitting on the patio with a small fire and a glass of wine.

Trimarked is CK's debut novel, and is the first of more to come. To keep tabs on future books, you can find her on social media and at her website, www.cksorens.com.

facebook.com/cksorens

instagram.com/ck_sorens

Made in the USA
Las Vegas, NV
05 June 2021

24243593R00125